Co-Winner of the 16th Annual International 3-Day Novel Writing Contest . . .

Stolen Voices

by

Steve R. Lundin

ANVIL PRESS

STOLEN VOICES
Copyright © 1994 Steve Lundin

Published by Anvil Press
Suite 204-A 175 East Broadway
Vancouver, B.C., CANADA
V5T 1W2

CANADIAN CATALOGUING IN PUBLICATION DATA

Lundin, Steve.
  Stolen voices / Steve Lundin. Vacant Rooms / Mitch Parry

  ISBN: 1-895636-06-X

  I. Parry, Mitch, 1960- Vacant rooms. II. Title. III. Title: Vacant rooms.

PS8573.U543S7 1994   C813'.54   C94-910089-7
PR9199.3.L86S7 1994

Typesetting: Anvil Press.

Cover Design: Greg White Illustration & Design.

Flip this book over for a second 3-Day Novel.

To Starving Artists

Book One

Children of Cain

CHAPTER ONE

Alizarin crimson, the blood of virgins, just a hint of a smear, there, between her legs and against the folds of alabaster gown. Skewing the scales, nudged by the gargoyle's shoulder, the muscle bunched as the beast cups her right breast.

Tod Coll tilted his head to one side. Its shadow, mane tangled, commanded a corner of the canvas—he'd angled the light just right, maintaining his presence. Things like that were getting important.

He heard steps on the stairs, and the thump of heels. Goren O'Dell heaving his bulk upward to the hallway, breathing hard with the burden of his night's supper. The thump of heels, now on the landing, now being dragged down the hall to the door past Tod's. Keys jangled, then Goren pulled his meal inside.

Tod closed his eyes. The walls were cardboard thin. He heard buttons scatter across the floor, the tearing of fabric, a wet, yielding sound, then Goren chewing: bones crunching, blood dripping heavy rhythm on the tile floor.

Tod opened his eyes and shook himself. Neighbours. He returned his attention to his painting, to what he'd seen this afternoon, there in front of Justice Hall. A gargoyle shinnying down one of the Greek columns beside the wide glass doors. Swift pad of soundless taloned feet to the side of Lady Justice, the poor woman blindfolded and her hands full. The gargoyle groped her, pausing for a lewd wink at Tod as he hurried past.

He stabbed his brush into some fresh yellow ochre.

Mindfulness was everything. Too easy to let go and there'd be trouble for sure. All that eye contact worked to keep him here. Maintained his presence. That gargoyle's wink had been a relief.

The wall thumped. Goren throwing bones again. Eating made him angry, a pacing fury exploding every now and then through the night. Splitting the bones for the marrow wasn't enough—he pounded them to pulp. Get to the brain through the face, never mind the mess, Dam Gigi would clean up in the morning, she always cleaned up in the morning. Gotta keep on top of things, she'd say, jabbing at Tod's face with her mop, else they get outa hand, but damn, O'Dell must've been on some kinda bender last night, eh?

The pate of the gargoyle's skull, a single turn with the brush. A dab of toilet paper, lay in that whitish sheen.

The phone rang. Tod grabbed it. "What?" In the room beyond everything had gone quiet. Goren's red eyes hooded now, suspicious, his wide nostrils testing the air.

"Painting, are we?" Bernard's heh-heh an asthmatic wheeze.

"So I'm painting."

"It's not the same old shit, is it? What about filling that order from Parlez—you got their cheque, didn't you? They want more of your pastorals, you know."

"Only because they don't know what's under 'em," Tod said. "Yeah, I got the cheque. Big deal."

"If you just settled on a style, you know, it'd make my job a damn sight easier, Tod."

"Big deal."

"You're painting one of those nightmare things, aren't you? I can tell. And now you'll probably cover most of it up. Titanium white, isn't it? You know how bloody hard it is selling white paintings?"

"*Calcined*, that's the style. I looked the word up. Calcined. Like when something, uhm, oxidises. The chemicals change and it turns white. Calcined, Bernard, that's the style."

"Fuck the style. You're making things hard on yourself. On me, too. Pastorals, Tod. Do more pastorals for Parlez—they're eating them up down there, bloody retired Yanks with Town Lincolns and big dens. You looked outside lately?"

"What?"

"It's that storm again. It's back, just hanging out to sea—ever tried looking out your fucking window, Tod? You know, the real world? Pastorals. Give me some pastorals by week's end."

Tod hung up. He stared at his canvas. Lady Justice, the gargoyle, the texture and the feeling up, the victim's blindfold and torn gown. Ready to paint over. Ready to calcine. But not now. Bernard Frank's call had left a bad taste in his mouth.

Through the wall the steady pacing resumed.

Tod rose and walked over to the window. Warehouses blocked most of his view, but he could see the upper edge of the storm cloud, the tiny figures of those frightening women soaring on updraughts. And there, within the cloud, *something*. Massive, towering, arms spread wide, flickering with lightning playing like sheets along its limbs. What might be waving hair, black and wild. It was closer tonight, a fraction closer.

Tod found his jacket at the foot of the bed. He pulled it on, studying the familiar angles, planes and shadows of his single room, canvases stacked in jagged piles, spent paint tubes crowded like dead worms around the waste-bin beside the desk. Stained drywall and a few shreds of blue wallpaper framing the thermostat.

He didn't bother locking the door behind him.

•   •   •

TWIN FURROWS RAN a wobbly track down the hall, leading to Goren O'Dell's door. Tod headed for the landing, stepping carefully. Bad luck, crossing those lines. From the main floor below rose the vaguely hysterical chatter of the night's crowd, punctuated by Gil's sneering call from the table by the stairs.

Tod descended the steps, headed straight ahead instead of to the left—Goren's route from the back alley—and entered Stalker's Bar.

"Mr. Painter! Get a fuckin' haircut, man." Gil was on his throne, the table before him laid out like an altar. Sharkskin suit and Arabic jewelry, smooth olive face and bright black eyes. He raised his glass of sherry as Tod walked by. "Fuckin' Mr. Painter, how's it hangin' man?"

"Who's writing your script, Gil?" Tod moved past, winding around a few of Gil's girls.

"Watch the merchandise, little man," Gil warned. "One of them's new, squeaky clean new, man."

Tod paused, swung his full attention to the girls. Easy to find her, barely fifteen and already strung out. Looking tough for her old high school but small here in Stalker's.

"You want first crack?" Gil asked.

"You get first crack," Tod replied, moving on. "And after you what's left?" Same question every time, same answer.

Gil laughed. "Fuckin' right, man. You got that right! Quality control, man, that's what I call it."

At the far end of the bar, near the doors, Death leaned his lanky skeletal frame on the counter. Even with the black robe Tod could see through most of him. Just another bloody regular at Stalker's, his scythe out for the straights and gays and the hypes hovering like wraiths outside. Death swung his gaze over as Tod approached, raising his Manhattan.

"Here's to patience, Mr. Coll."

"When it's all you got."

Tod stepped out into the city's midnight chill. The wraiths eyed him hollowly, despairing of the familiar when it meant no luck. They slipped to either side as he passed. Opposite the alley Tod paused. The Kid was there, hunched in the shadows, surrounded by mangy dogs. The Kid passed out scraps of food. The Kid—Gil's naming—probably weighed a good two-fifty, all of it muscle, stood at a round-shouldered and stooped six and a half feet, hairy as an ape. Looking into the Kid's eyes made Tod think of Africa, though he'd never been there, and the Kid was white-skinned under all the hair and dirt. Herds and watering holes, a dip of the shaggy head at dawn, tenuous draught, ears pricked.

He lived in the alleys, and whimpered when it rained, until the strays gathered around him with the gift of warmth.

Tod gave the Kid a nod, then moved on. Couldn't open a door for the boy—he'd run the other way. Gil kept him fed and called it adoption.

The storm cloaked the horizon, flickers of lightning unveiling the flying women and whatever drove them on, momentary flashes of revelation that shivered through Tod, dancing cold fire along his bones. Sometimes he could almost hear them—the wind-whipped women shrieking endless songs, as if cursed with music. Sometimes he heard his name.

The city was still, the air motionless; few cars and a low fog on the streets. He strode through the pleasant darkness, hunching his shoulders against the distant roar of the Skytrain as it circled the city, above the fog, lit windows like bared teeth. Tod hated the Skytrain, hated its elevated pride, the way it circled and circled, head hunting tail. Some manic adoration of the future, some call to things not yet modern. Sheer new. Succumbing to convenience like everything else did these days. Here in the race against nothing, head hunting tail.

The park gates hung ajar—a good sign. Tod entered the closed-in path, the air heavy with the sweat of the trees. He passed the bronze statue, ignoring the creak of its head as it swung its pitted gaze on him. Damn thing never had anything to say anyway, too busy gripping its cock in silent, perfect commentary on modern art. Tod admired the artist's honesty, if not her taste.

He could smell the pond before seeing it through the trees. Sweet and weighty with duck shit, pumps full of feathers and algae. Still and silent, thallo green and muddy umber.

The path took a turn, opened out to reveal the pond, the lone bench, and the four men seated on it. Sig to the right, on his lap the wallet full of snapshots—the blonde bombshell who got away and would you know it, gentlemen? Hitched up to some Hun can you believe that?

Beside him sat Rolly, his black sports jacket buttoned top two only, please. Rolly, who'd fought in the war, stood firm on the Maginot line even though the Nazis went around it this time, being uncultured and coarse. Then George, quiet and lost, who kept a dead crow in his pocket which he threw at the pigeons when they got too close. Putting a space between himself and the others, not easy with the four of them on that bench, sat Art, scowling and bitter, hating children and scaring them from the bushes, with a curse for every mother who dared challenge him.

The pressure of the storm behind him slowly eased as Tod approached. The four men were plucking ducks. Pale white, bony bodies lay scattered around the bench, some still twitching. Sig was talking.

"Can you believe that? Sure it was just a glimmer, but I saw her white knuckles through the slime, gentlemen, closed on the hilt. Evening, Mr. Coll—as I was just saying, I saw her today. This afternoon, in fact. Just a glimmer, of course."

"It's his eyes, Tod," said Rolly, plucking a feather from his pebbled nose. "They're dysfunctional, a common ailment, of course."

"Kill the poets," Art said quietly, wringing another duck's neck.

Rolly leaned back and wiped his hands on his thighs. "Ah," he said, "I see George smiling. Just a matter of faith, is it? Well, you and Sig are welcome to sit here for the rest of your days. I've a mind to leave, once and for all, and Art can take his homilies to the bank."

Tod picked up a naked duck. "Mind if I take one?"

Rolly tossed up his hands. "As many as you like, Tod! God knows we don't eat them."

The duck fit neatly into his coat pocket. Tod collected

another one. "I was hoping you'd get tired of pigeons, sooner or later," he said, collecting a third for the inside pocket. "Rats with wings, and they taste it."

"No doubt," Rolly said. "Well," he swiftly rose and smoothed out his pants. "She's waiting," he nodded at the pond, "and the war's over now, isn't it? No more walls to man, barricades to defend—Hitler spoiled all that now, didn't he? He did what the world does these days: moves fast and around and eats you from the inside out. I'm off for the swan."

Tod took his place on the bench. They watched Rolly march away into a grove of trees.

"In the mists of dawn," Art said softly, "the betrayers all covered in dew."

"It's your own fault," Sig muttered.

The old stories, hashed and rehashed, a deep plough tugging up memories of war on some battlefield. Helms and greaves and broken hearts. Tod liked to sit here, in the company of old men, as they waited before the pond for some unknown mistress. Vying for the lady's regard, seated in perpetual obedience. They were familiar, friends who shared the darkness and maybe saw things the way Tod saw things. Maybe. He wasn't sure, but it didn't really matter— they just took Tod as he was, a weathered, short, thin man of forty-eight with a head of iron hair and a frightened look in his watery blue eyes.

Tod had tried the self-portraits. Mindfulness, maintaining your presence. Like Andre Narcisse and his sixty-two self-portraits in the Gallery of Art. But frightened men didn't sell, frightened men made people look away. Not like Narcisse's *let's fuck in the foyer* face. Confidence of the supreme sort, making the world simple and small and barely worth the sneering turn of his full lips.

It comforted. Neo-post-colonial-ethnic-post-modernism. Shock or soothe, eye to eye in the game of evasion. Of those who could see, few left. Fewer and fewer, ready for the post-mortem discovery—when all was safe and the haunted hand was forever still.

Pastorals.

Art reached for another duck. "Kill the poets," he said.

CHAPTER TWO

The doors of Paternal Trust opened at 10:05. Duck heads dangling from his pockets, Tod made his way to the front of the longest line. No one objected.

Another busy morning for the tellers, their white faces and purple lips turning into ghastly smiles for each new customer they invited forward. Tod watched the man being served, the same man he always saw. A fine business suit and a monk's crown of thin brown hair, the stubbly pebbles on the back of his neck, the wide flat hands on the counter as the teller and the computer challenged each other. Fingers with thick wedding band and something all covered in diamonds. Gold watch black-faced, perfect cuffs and briefcase like a patient dog next to his leather wing-tips.

Red stains marred the teller's mouth and chin. Stains in various measures for all the tellers. Tod craned his head and looked beyond the booth, finding the Manager's office. Door closed as usual. Mahogany and buttoned black leather, the door that said Mr. Sanguire, Manager, Paternal Trust. Closed closed closed.

The businessman said something to the teller. The teller said something back. The businessman looked away for a moment, rounded profile and lined jowls, then looked back and said something else as he gathered up his chequebook, pen and credit card. The teller—young, thin body, thin neck, a mass of auburn hair—licked her purple lips.

The businessman hurried away.

Tod stepped up to the booth and slapped his cheque on the counter. "Cash." He watched the taloned fingers probe forward under the plexiglass, spear the cheque and draw it back. "The name's Tod Coll. I've got an account here. Had it here for ten years. Never bounced nothing. Cash."

"This is a U.S. cheque, Mr. Coll. Your account number?"

He told her, watched as she worked the keyboard. He knew the balance. Thirty-three dollars. He watched as the usual veil of something dead slipped over her blood-shot eyes. She licked her lips.

"I'm sorry, Mr. Coll. This cheque will require a thirty day hold."

"It's from Parlez Gallery, in Tucson, Arizona. Where all the old people live. It's a big gallery. We go through this every time I bring in a cheque from them. Five years of this, Miss. Thirty day holds and every cheque good, Miss."

"I'm sorry."

"Let me see the Manager."

"You'll need an appointment."

"I'll make one."

"Mr. Sanguire won't be in today, I'm afraid."

"He's in right now. I can see him through that stained glass beside the door. In his office right now. Let me see him."

"Shall I provisionally deposit your cheque?"

"Fuck off."

He snatched his cheque from her cold hands and stalked out of the bank. Same old shit. Five years. Ten years. He didn't even know what Mr. Sanguire looked like.

Outside in the warm sunshine, Tod hesitated. He felt tired, a deep weariness settling in his shoulders. He hated the ritual to come. Same old shit. Maybe it could wait an hour or two.

People streamed past. Cars and buses and taxis and trucks in the street. Seers with shopping carts and warlocks with upturned hats on the corners. Winged rats hunting bread crumbs on the broad sidewalk near the fountain across the street. Skytrain circling.

Pastorals.

Tod swung left and made his way to the Gallery of Art. The sidewalk was crowded, but he walked a straight line. Men had their briefcases and he had his ducks. No contest. The Gallery was a massive blockish building bereft of style in the hopes of not offending anyone. It commanded a corner of City Square, kitty-corner from Justice Hall. The blindfolded Lady faced it from her pedestal outside Justice Hall, with gargoyle shadows edging ever closer behind her.

Tod climbed the steps and pushed open the glass doors. An eight by ten foot Andre Narcisse smirked at him. Tod hesitated, jolted off-balance by the new display. He shook himself, glanced over at the reception desk beyond the next set of glass doors. She was out for coffee, her station empty for the next few minutes. Like clockwork.

He pulled a rolled sheet of paper from his inside pocket. Feathers drifted around on the air conditioner's aimless currents. A bottle of glue with a wide brush came out of another pocket. He went to the Events case and brushed thick smears of glue onto the glass. He unrolled the paper and carefully tamped it down. Even, no air bubbles—they'd need a paint scraper to get it off, and even then it wouldn't be easy.

Tod entered the gallery's main hall, hurried past the reception desk and made his way into the Exhibits chambers.

Jim Smithers, alias Andre Narcisse.

Narcisse putting a banana up his anus. Narcisse fucking a mirror. Narcisse buried up to his chin in large unattached female breasts. Narcisse climbing into a giant vagina. Narcisse's face on a pregnant belly. Narcisse on a throne with serpentine women slithering toward him. Narcisse laughing all the way to Paternal Trust.

Tod's head spun as he stumbled out of Exhibits. Jim Smithers, a terrified commercial artist with the ache of need in every bone. Jim Smithers, who mistrusted comfort and nursed a bleeding ulcer behind his penthouse desk. Billboard Smithers. Eat drink smoke buy satisfy multiply get high. Savings earnings winnings. Watch attend come on down.

He'd come by and talk, late hours in Tod's cramped room. All the aches needing a voice, needing an ear. Stay away from acrylic, Tod said. Christ, it's *plastic paint!* Stick with oils, even water colours. Mineral pigments—they remind us of where it all started, in some fucking cave in France, Jim. Forget the Indians, forget the Africans, forget the Japanese. You're white and Europe's it for you. Never sneer at what you are, where you came from. The Indians don't sneer—they celebrate. Nothing's as old as those cave paintings, Jim. That's your tradition. Celebrate it.

I know, all we're doing these days is stomping on it. We don't think it's good enough. Think it's boring. Give us the exotic anytime. Grab something from the jungle and stick it on a wall in a glass and concrete building.

Fuck juxtaposition, Jim. Big word for wrongness.

Scrambles our sense of what's right, that's all. A cheap aesthetic high.

Jim Smithers, who took the plunge, but brought his cape and suit with him, one slick downward swoop with fanfare and mystery. Sell first, produce later. Give me image or give me death.

The nightly visits ended. Andre Narcisse used bed springs, sofa stuffing, condoms, pubic hair, acrylic. African, Indian, Polynesian, Japanese, Chinese, Arabic, Inuit motifs. Stolen styles and stolen voices.

Fear answered his need, gave him a silent self. Freed him to hide behind other tongues, other eyes, other hands. He took his tradition and narrowed it down to his own face, then fucked it.

Made him famous. A millionaire.

Tod moved on, into the back rooms, where the old exhibits glowered from under bad light. The asylum, the works of those who could see. Both nightmares and dreams, ethics of courage and wonder. The air was dusty, smelling of amnesia, some wilful consignment of the profound in comfort's name.

He stood before his favourite work in the gallery. Some obscure Italian, 1897-1945. *Children of Cain*, oil on canvas, 1945 (the artist's last work). A mad-man's hand, losing more of himself with every brush stroke. Yellow ochre dominating, burnt sienna, burnt umber, cadmium yellow deep, cadmium red deep, alizarin crimson. Faces and figures, gargoyles, Goren O'Dells, four old men outside a dilapidated villa in front of a pond, a man sheathed in bestial hair running with jackals, a king surrounded by prostitutes, Hitler and Mussolini beating a chained swan, Stalin in a rowboat on a sea of blood, the tide sweeping him away. Figures and faces crowded inside the rough outlines of a mammoth on a wall of rock, the faint colours hinting at oil lamps and bracken torches smeared in tar.

"*No fucking in the Foyer.*"

Tod knew the voice behind him, and smiled. "You saw it?"

"Couldn't miss it. Right under Andre's name."

Tod didn't turn around. Johan Sacristi's presence behind him was a warm thing, a generous thing.

"Whenever I find you in the gallery," Johan said, "I find you here. The man was insane."

"So?"

"I hear your empathy, Tod. They call this room the asylum. They call the Main Hall pure brilliance."

"Narcisse."

"Is starving better?"

Tod turned away from *Children of Cain*. Johan was short, round, his narrow white collar yellowed along the rim. A tattered bible jutted from his coat pocket.

"I suppose you haven't heard," Johan said, eyeing the painting. "The city's having visitors from Rome."

"Why?"

Johan smiled. "You know why, Tod."

"What do you think they'll do to you?"

"Excommunication at best, I should think."

"Snapping the chains."

"Maybe." Johan walked over to the next painting, an earlier work by the same Italian. *Shrouding the Beast*, 1938, oil on canvas (prior to imprisonment). "What do you see?"

"A fearless man."

"As fearless as you, Tod?"

He shook his head. "I'm not fearless, Johan. I can never look too long."

"You have a name for it."

23

"Calcined."

"Oh yes. Some principle of oxidation. Like the cliffs of Dover."

"I have to cover it up."

"Seems extreme."

"I don't cover it all, though. Do I?"

Johan moved on to the next painting. "No," he said, drawing out the word. "You make revelation harder than it might be. Maybe that's where its value comes from."

"I can't sell them. I can't even show them."

"Not what I meant."

Tod followed him as he moved from one work to the next. The asylum was a crowded place, every wall cramped, sculptures narrowing the pathways. "Looking for inspiration?" Tod asked.

"I've never had an answer for why I come here."

"I thought maybe this time."

Johan turned bright, intense eyes on Tod. "Why now?"

Tod shrugged. "Your visitors from Rome."

"Ah."

They completed the circuit in silence. A few moments offered to each effort, each struggle. At the entranceway, both paused. Tod always left the asylum with a feeling of ritual, something completed, a sacred dance around the world's pitfalls. He wondered if Johan felt the same.

"Perhaps," said Johan, "we'll meet at the park tonight. I'm giving a public sermon."

"You got arrested last time."

Johan shrugged. "Part of the sermon."

"If I've got the time."

"Painting?"

"Covering up. I painted last night."

"Ah," Johan smiled. "I'd wondered why your eyes were so

clear today."

They parted ways outside the gallery. Tod crossed the square to Justice Hall. The gargoyle had come down from his perch, heatedly groping the Lady. Her gown was torn away at the front. The gargoyle had clambered up her, gripping the cloth with hands and feet, and now chewed eagerly at her nipples. The scales had twisted and hung in a snarl of knotted chain.

As Tod walked past, the gargoyle released one hand and waved.

Tod rushed up the steps and inside Justice Hall. Courtrooms to the right, Mayor's office to the left. He went left, through glass doors, down the hall, past the receptionist who stared at the duck heads dangling from his pockets for a moment too long, reaching for the phone as he approached the Mayor's door. He pushed it open in time to see the Mayor's secretary hang up her phone. She gave Tod a broad smile. Tod smiled back.

"Hi, Sue, Stephen in?"

"He is," she replied. "Hold a sec." She picked up the phone again.

Election fever. Just a tinge of it, but there, a sour smell of impending panic in the cool conditioned air. The palm tree beside Sue's desk was dying. Yellow ochre, a dab of black a dab of white, evenly mixed for the leaves.

"Head right in," Sue said, replacing the receiver.

Stephen Tyme's office still had the feel of that adolescent's room on the top floor of 51 Widowlark Lane, the track and field trophies, Paul Henderson's winning goal in Russia expensively framed, flanked by the SFU Law Degree, some kind of undergraduate degree, and the Dean's List for both schools—a minor discrepancy for a teenager's room, but absolute with intent.

Stephen sat behind his desk, talking on the phone. A red-spotted bandage marred his high tanned forehead, just above the left eye. He waved distractedly at Tod, motioning him to take a seat.

Tod turned and discovered another person in the office. A youngish woman, impeccably dressed, crisp zinc white and cobalt blue, legs crossed and hands folded on her lap. Sitting on the chair beside her was an expensive portfolio binder. She smiled up at Tod and slowly removed the portfolio, which she leaned against her own chair.

"Thanks." Tod sat down.

"Are those ducks?" she asked.

The voice reminded him of someone, deep for a woman, a hint of cool power behind the surface warmth.

"Supper," he answered. "I'm Tod Coll."

"Athenia Crane."

"Pleased to meet you."

Stephen's voice rose, catching their attention.

"Sky's the limit? Is that what you said? What kind of a fucking nauseating slogan is that? It's bloody beautiful, that's what it is, Bill! I don't care if he does decide to use it, he's toast." He paused for a long moment, looked up at Tod and Athenia and winked. "We go after him, Bill, you hear me? I don't care. I don't give a fucking flying leap. This is politics!" He hung up.

The grin he turned on Tod was feral. "One fucking year out of law school, and he's running for mayor!"

"Who?"

"My son, the little shit. Running against his old man, what the fuck's this world coming to? *Sky Tyme for Mayor! Sky's the limit! Vote Sky!* Jesus Christ!"

Athenia smiled. "You knew it was coming."

"Fuck that—I'll eat him alive."

There was an awkward pause. Frowning, Stephen abstractedly probed the bandage on his head. His gaze wandered a moment, then swung to Tod. "You met my daughter?"

Tod blinked, then turned to the woman beside him. "Oh, I guess so."

"Just one more headache," Stephen said.

"Gee, thanks, Dad."

"Too early for an election. I haven't greased enough palms yet. Sky's already at my throat, and now look who pops up—my long lost daughter."

"Well," Tod said, smiling at Athenia, "I've known your father since high school. And you're a mystery to me."

"That sounds nice."

"Long story," Stephen said. "So what brings you here, Tod? Oh, of course. Same old shit, eh?"

Tod pulled out the cheque. "Got a pen?"

He signed the cheque over to Stephen.

"Sue will have the money by this afternoon, usual time."

"Great," Tod said. "Thanks."

"No problem. Christ, go buy a roast, and some potatoes. Those ducks are getting high."

Tod rose.

Stephen winked at Athenia, then leaned back in his chair. "So what's this I hear about a show at the Gallery of Art? About fucking time, Tod."

"What show?"

"Got a call from Bernard Frank, your agent, right? Said you're into a new style these days. Marketable. Asked me to pull some strings, since you and me go back, right?"

"What new style?"

Stephen grinned. "Had a feeling. Fucking agents, eh? Well, you got the show if you want it. But the schedule's tight, so hop to it. None of that white stuff, either. Find something new, kick 'em in the balls. Sounds good, right? Drop by for a drink sometime. Not tomorrow, though. Got to meet some Archbishops from Rome. I think they're Archbishops. Big stiff robes, anyway, real ceremony shit. Day after tomorrow should do. Don't spend it all in one place, Tod. Eight grand U.S. should last you a month, easy. Call Sue in on your way out. *Sky's the limit!* Fuck me! I'll eat him alive."

Athenia followed Tod out.

"What's in the portfolio," he asked as they left Sue's office.

"Nothing. I just bought it."

"Oh. Well, what do you plan on putting in it?"

"Not sure, yet. I'll think of something."

"You paint? Draw? Take pictures?"

"No."

"Is it a fashion accessory?"

"Like your ducks?"

"That eight grand's got to last me all year."

"I figured that."

They reached the foyer. Athenia paused, eyes on the courtrooms.

"Nice meeting you," Tod said.

"And you."

"Never knew Stephen had a daughter. Where you been hiding?"

"In his head. Bye."

He watched her stride into the courtrooms. "Explains the bandage," he muttered.

Book Two

Shrouding the Beast

CHAPTER THREE

Tod stared at the painting. He'd laid out the titanium white on a sheet of cardboard beside him, mixed in the loose linseed oil. A wad of toilet paper in his right hand. Ready to start.

The gargoyle's face leered at him above the shadow of his own head, a mocking progeny. Groping, ready with a wink and a wave. From somewhere below came Gil's wild laughter.

Something held him back, something like courage, or madness. He felt ready to face that gargoyle, face the degrading act that mimed the misery of mankind, an act played out in the safe, lofty places of the intellect where visions of mastery and power ruled unchallenged. Painting empty craft had its place, an artist's moment away from struggle. A place to flee toward, then from.

He wanted to throttle that gargoyle.

Footsteps sounded on the stairs, heavy, but unencumbered. Tod didn't recognise them. Holding his breath, he waited.

The knock made him jump. He rose swiftly, almost lurching back from the painting, a reason to escape amidst the sucking gulp of courage down the drain. A moment at the door, then. A moment, then the titanium white.

The knock sounded again as he reached the door. Irritated, he flung it open.

Before him stood a giant of a man, neatly dressed in a blue pin-stripe suit. He held a large black leather briefcase, the kind teachers used to carry. Square jaw clean shaven, wavy reddish-blonde hair reaching the collar; massive hands massively scarred. The man's mouth smiled, his blue eyes withholding all warmth.

"Good evening, sir. My name is Robert Geat."

"So?"

"Do you know the love of God?"

"I sleep alone, as far as I can tell. Look, I'm in the middle of something."

"Aren't we all?"

"What the hell does that mean?"

Robert Geat's smile dropped, a bewildered look claiming his face.

"Lost in your own profundity, huh?"

The man recovered, that deadly look back in his eyes. "I think, Mr. O'Dell, we'd best talk inside."

Tod's laugh was harsh. "You got the wrong guy. O'Dell lives next door, and he isn't home yet."

"I see." Robert Geat looked around, bemused.

"Is he expecting you?"

The eyes returned to him.

Tod almost reeled, falling into that even, depthless gaze. He gripped the door-frame and looked away.

Robert Geat spoke, "I'll try later, then."

"Right," Tod managed. "Bye." He closed the door.

Titanium white, he moved for it like an addict.

• • •

DAM GIGI SAT rocking at the foot of the stairs. Tod stepped around her, intent on a stiff drink at the bar, then he hesitated.

"Something wrong?"

The large woman raised her lined, puffy face and regarded him with red-rimmed eyes. "I don't know the love of God, Mr. Coll. That's what he said. I don't know the love of God. And he's coming back. I know he is. I know it!"

Tod crouched down beside her. "What if he does?"

She dropped her face back into her broad hands. "You don't know, Mr. Coll. You just don't know."

He looked around, wondering what to say. The stairs leading to the basement were halfway down the hall. Dam Gigi lived down there, somewhere. "Listen," he said, laying an arm over her shoulders. "How about I take you back to your room. Better than these stairs, right? I'll make you a cup of tea."

"Better a belt," she said.

"Got enough for two?"

"Okay," she said, climbing upright. "That'd be nice."

The stairs started straight, then wound into a steep spiral; after the first floor beneath ground level, they changed from wood to stone. The air felt wet, stale.

They continued down for another five minutes, at one point passing a section where the stone walls glowed with some kind of mould, luminous spots of yellow light that seemed to swim in tight circles when Tod paused for a closer look.

Dam Gigi led him to a heavy wooden door with a simple

wrought iron latch. She smiled shyly over her shoulder, then entered.

Tod followed, his steps slowing as he looked around in wonder. A single room, its ceiling lost in darkness, lit only by thick tallow candles. Furs on the floor, mostly bear from the look of them. At the chamber's far end, opposite the door, the entire wall was hidden behind a pile of antique furniture. The pile was ten feet high, maybe more. Looked to be worth a fortune.

Dam Gigi walked over to the brick-lined hearth in the centre of the room and tossed a piece of fence post onto the embers. "Got a bottle of the good stuff on that shelf over there," she said. "Find yourself a chair and sit here by the fire, 'gainst the chill. I'll find us some cups." She started rummaging through a steamer chest.

Tod found the shelf, and a large clay bottle that swished when he shook it. To one side stood a cup, dulled brass. He reached for it. "Found one cup, anyway," he said.

"Not that one!" she snapped.

Tod pulled his hand back. "Okay." He carried the bottle back to the hearth. The fence post had ignited, radiating light and warmth. The smoke seemed to rise up through a flue somewhere directly above the fire. Dam Gigi returned with two plastic cups.

"Didn't mean to make you jump," she said.

Tod pulled the cork and poured. The liquor was amber in colour, smelling sweet. "That's all right."

"That's a special cup. I'm saving it for him."

Tod thought to ask who, then changed his mind. "This stuff smells like honey."

"Yep," she said.

They both drank. The mead burned down Tod's throat; he fought back a cough, then sat back as heat swept through him. "Uhm."

"Aren't we all God's children?" she asked, a hint of the earlier moaning in her tone. "That man said I was forsaken, a damnation, he said."

"A fanatic," Tod said. "Never mind him. You'd be surprised who purports to speak for God."

"Purports?"

"Pretends."

"He said he had witnesses."

"Witnesses?"

"God and a poet, he said. His witnesses. Before God and the poet, he said, I shall defend righteousness."

"The guy's a nutter, if you ask me. Top up your cup?"

"He said was looking for Goren. I asked why, but he wouldn't say. What would he want with Goren?"

"No idea," Tod said.

After the third cup she was asleep in her chair. Tod found a blanket in a chest and draped it over her. He was half-drunk himself and had to fight the illusion that the stairs were marching down while he marched up, like some fated journey without end.

Winded and dizzy, he finally reached the main floor. He paused at the door to Stalker's, took a few deep breaths, then entered.

"Hey Mr. Painter! Come to tie one on?" Gil's laugh a hoarse bray.

"How about around your neck?" Tod answered, walking past.

"Funny little man, watch the merchandise."

Low thunder rolled in from the distant storm, seeming to come from somewhere under Tod's feet. He stepped up to the bar. Faint singing came on the thunder, voices that might be calling his name. He shook his head.

"Buy you a beer, Mr. Coll?"

Tod glanced over as Death sidled up beside him. "Is this the fatal sip, then?"

"Admittedly the draft is somewhat stale, but you'll survive it."

"Fine, only I don't really need your charity tonight."

"Of course."

Tod caught the bartender's eye. "A draft and a Manhattan, Edward."

"Damned fine combination, mon. Cho." Edward headed for the mixing station, snagging a bottle of bourbon as he went.

In the mirror Tod watched Gil stride over to the alley door, fling it open in time to catch the Kid collecting his latest offering—a half dozen hamburgers. The Kid ducked under the harsh light and Gil roared with laughter. Dogs scattered into the alley's shadows. The Kid collected the last hamburger and lumbered out of sight.

"Poor Gil," Death murmured. "He'll never get what he wants."

"And what's that? Chastity?"

"I wait at the end of all your aspirations."

"Sounds dramatic." Tod downed a mouthful of beer, the taste bitter after the mead.

"Mostly pathetic," Death said. "You understand, of course, that the storm wants you. That it's coming for you, and there's nothing you can do to stop it. Short of dying, that is."

"Thought I heard my name," Tod said, staring at his pale face in the mirror.

"This doesn't frighten you?"

"Terrifies me."

"It comes for those who can see, Mr. Coll."

He heard a distant sliding moan—the Skytrain, swinging close. "You'd think we'd get a break or two, wouldn't you?"

"I'd like to attend your gallery opening."

"I'll put you on the invitation list."

CHAPTER FOUR

Tod stood at the transactions counter, waiting for a pallid man to get off the phone. The businessman was softly arguing with one of the tellers off to Tod's right, too distant to make out any words, but the teller kept licking her lips, leaning forward as if held taut by an invisible tether. Other tellers slowly closed in on the scene.

The pallid man hung up, slowly rose, and walked over. "Can I help you?"

"I'd like to see Mr. Sanguire."

"Do you have an appointment?"

"Yes."

"Your name, sir?"

"Tod Coll."

"One moment, please." The man walked over to the leather door, knocked on the frame, then slipped inside. Over at the other counter the businessman's voice was getting louder. The teller had bared her teeth.

Raw fear gripped Tod. He felt it now, an air of impending frenzy. The other tellers were closing in, mouths hanging open. The line waiting behind the businessman started backing away, moving for the doors. The teller's canines framed her purple bottom lip.

"Trouble with incoming this month," the businessman's voice thin and getting plaintive. "Just a few more days, if Mr. Sanguire will allow—"

"Mr. Sanguire," the pallid man said, his eyes on the scene at the wicket, "has no record of your appointment." He licked his lips, fingers clutching and opening. "However, he always has time for a friend of Mayor Tyme. If you'll . . . " The man voiced a soft snarl and jerked toward his fellow tellers.

Tod took a step back, his heart hammering in his chest. Customers broke for the doors. The businessman screamed, grabbing his briefcase and lurching away from the wicket. The teller had clambered over the plexiglass. As the businessman turned to run, she leapt at his back.

Blood sprayed across the marble floor. The other tellers closed in, including the man from transactions. Tod jumped as a heavy thump shook the door to Mr. Sanguire's office. A high pitched keening sounded dimly from behind it, then frantic battering.

Tod backed to the far wall. The businessman crawled for the door, leaving his intestines behind in a tumbled, flopping sprawl. The tellers dug their claws into his back and thighs, dragging him into their arms. His screaming fell to a slow moan, then silence as the tellers began feeding. A few raised stained faces in Tod's direction.

He made his way, slowly, to the doors, their red eyes tracking him. A moment later his groping hand found the door handle.

The sunshine seemed unnaturally bright, the air unbearably hot. Streams of people swung past him as he stood outside Paternal Trust. After a long moment he turned around and squarely faced the bank. People in, people out, a current of unperturbed humanity. Tod rubbed at his eyes.

Mindfulness. The practice of *pastoralism*. Keep a grip on things, a sense of presence. Across from him the gargoyle had his hands between the Lady's legs, a steady pushing motion that whipped the scales in wild arcs. Down the street a dozen witches burned a housewife at the stake. A roar made him turn in time to see the Skytrain emerge from the storm cloud, streaming black tendrils from its gaping mouth.

Tod staggered down the street. He came to a phone stall, found a quarter and frantically dialled. One ring, two . . .

"Bernard Frank Agencies, can I help you?"

"It's Tod."

"Been trying to get a hold of you, Tod! What's with this fucking disappearing act? Listen, your buddy the Mayor's come through—how's twelve grand sound? A special grant for one of the city's own, or something like that. We got an appointment at his office tomorrow, 10 a.m. sharp. Got that?"

"I'll do it," Tod said. "A new series. Pastorals . . . "

"Pastorals like hell, Tod! This is the Gallery of *Art* we're talking about here. I said a new style, Tod. Something utterly fucking new, Magnum .44-to-their-heads-stuff."

"I don't—I don't know what . . . "

"Inspiration, Tod! Find it, and find it now! This is big time, none of that fucking fragile ego artsy-fartsy shit. That twelve grand's just a drop, Tod, a fucking shake of the prick. We'll eat Narcisse alive! Talk to you later, bye."

Numbed, Tod started walking.

He stepped around a man wearing a hide loincloth. Someone had nailed him to the sidewalk. A cup hovered over his head, dripping acid. The man's screams chased Tod around the corner.

Two ravens waited for him at the park gates.

"Mind the mistletoe," one said as he passed. The other hopped down and kept pace.

"Goes back to the Indo-Europeans, if you'll recall, Mr. Coll. Northern India, that cow after the flood, just floating down." The raven flapped forward a few yards as Tod sped up. The bird landed and resumed. "Can you do the Shiva, Mr. Coll? It's an old two-step. Popular at the last apocalypse. Jog anything in that head of yours? You know, archetypes— I'm just trying to be helpful."

"Go away."

The raven stopped, watching forlornly as Tod hurried past.

He came to the pond, to the bench. Tod slowed. No one there. Then he heard shouts from a nearby grove, the hissing of a goose. A moment later Sig and Rolly stumbled backward from the bushes. Armed with spears, they jabbed at the bird as it lunged into view. Art came after the goose, limping. He saw Tod and waved, then pointed toward the bench. George was sitting there now, hunched forward, forearms on thighs, gaze steady on the pond.

The goose darted between Sig and Rolly, honked once then took to the air. Sig threw his spear, missed.

Everyone converged on George at the bench.

"Like the Nazis," Rolly said, wiping his brow. "Never sit still, always this way then that. Linguistic origin of goose-stepping, one would suppose. Good afternoon, Tod."

"Inspiration."

"Bad timing," Rolly said, sitting down beside George. "I've a mind to leave this fiasco. Once and for all."

"I almost hit him," Sig said. "Did you see? Less than an

inch. Can you believe my luck?" He pulled out his wallet and sat down, suddenly morose. "Can you believe my luck?" he asked again in a quiet tone.

"Kill the children," Art said. "A simple command, guaranteed to solve the world's problems. An answer to our pain, Mr. Coll, don't you understand? No children, no mothers. No mothers, no betrayal. But the poet heard, he heard."

"We're all waiting," George said, startling everyone. "That's all." He looked up at Tod. "When she comes, the waiting will end."

Tod stared down at the four of them. Four luckless old men. He turned away.

"Can you believe my luck?" Sig said.

Art started crying. "Kill the children, I commanded. That's all."

• • •

THE TERMINAL'S CROWDS ebbed and waned. Tod stood at the top of the stairs, as close as he'd ever come, watching the Skytrain hiss forward, come to a halt, doors sliding open, gorging and disgorging.

In each one he saw Athenia Crane, with her portfolio, sitting there in the first car, watching him. She went uptown, then downtown, watching him steadily, something stern and protective in her expression, her portfolio raised like a shield.

Tod clutched his Day Pass, moving it from one hand to the other. Inspiration, into the beast's sleek belly. He didn't know what else to do.

Along the skyline, out over the harbour, the storm edged closer, flickering, rumbling, women singing and that massive, hungry shape, veiled by the writhing clouds. Arms flashing white, bangles glittering on the wrists, fingernails curving talons painted gold. Sweet yellow ochre, a touch of cadmium yellow deep. A woman, he knew that now. A woman, the empty cavern in his life, a woman who could see.

Maybe.

The Skytrain returned. Heading out of the city. Tod pushed himself into motion, walked on stiff legs for the nearest open doorway. Was she here? He stepped inside, and found himself alone in the first car.

The doors slid shut. Tod turned full circle, then laughed out loud. Finding inspiration in others was a dangerous thing, something he'd always known, something George had been telling him. He sat down.

He watched the city unravel. Out into some mysterious hinterland full of salt marshes and piers. Then beyond, leaning into a slow, steady curve over jagged mountains that opened out onto prairie, farmhouses like chips of coloured paper, tilled rows of hopeful earth, endless lakes and railway tracks winding through sap green forests. Lakes as big as seas, dun brown, then deep cobalt blue. Passing distant cities, out over the ocean dotted with icebergs, then an island, winding between stones standing in heather, across a narrow channel wracked by fierce winds, more standing stones, these ones squat and in threes, buttresses and lintels. Sweeping down into twisting caves, past dim shapes on the mouldy walls. Bison, cats, pregnant horses, and out again, high above steppes and desert, strange stepped pyramids rising from fields littered with abandoned war machines. Over a warm, soft-looking ocean, then through islands glittering with cities. A massive spanse of becalmed water, to a rugged coastline with a harbour crowded with tankers, then downtown.

The doors slid open. Tod walked out, back at the same terminal. The storm looked closer, the woman's arms opening wide for him.

• • •

THE CAVALCADE ENDED at St. Michael's. Three short men in stiff brocaded robes and high hats emerged from the limo and shook hands with Mayor Stephen Tyme. The crowd cheered and waved. Stephen waved back, then accompanied the three men up to the doors of St. Michael's.

Hands in his pockets, Tod watched from across the street. Four policemen on motorcycles waited in front of the Mayor's limo, dressed in black with skull-like helmets. One periodically tested the edge of his scythe—he looked familiar under all that leather.

"The Mayor did that well, didn't he?"

"Johan. I thought you'd be inside."

The small round man ran a hand through his hair. "Not yet. Time for deliberations, a slow mounting of tension if you will."

"Sorry I missed your last sermon."

"I was thinking of one on the steps of the gallery. Something about ethics and art, quoting Dostoevsky and Tolstoy."

"Obsolete notions," Tod said. "I read that in a magazine."

"Ah, well. Beats free will."

The men in robes disappeared inside St. Michael's. Mayor Stephen Tyme waved one last time, then went back to his limo, climbed inside, and drove off, the policemen flanking.

"Is that why they're here, then?" Tod asked. "Your sermons on free will?"

"And freedom from guilt." Johan paused, his eyes on St.

Michael's doors. "I expect they'll wilfully restrain my freedom, conclude the crime's committal, then string me up for my guilt."

"You could walk away, Johan."

A sharp glance, something skittering in his eyes. "So could you, Tod. Besides, we both know—you end up facing the music no matter which way you turn. Art and ethics, Tod, a sermon to keep in mind, I think." He looked at his watch. "Ah, fifteen minutes to agree on the exact wording. Time to go."

Tod watched his friend cross the street, a dull sense of dread spreading through him.

CHAPTER FIVE

Tod cleared his desk, set a new canvas on its stained and pitted surface. He stared down at the blank weave, his body slowly surrendering motion, falling into empty stillness.

Thunder shook the room, rattling the brushes in the tin can. From behind the wall came the creak of Goren's bed. Awake, finally, rising for the night's hunt. Tod sighed, a sense of normalcy returning to him.

He listened as Goren thumped to the door, closing his enormous gnarled hand on the tiny doorknob, turning it, stepping out into the hall.

Tod almost missed the other footsteps, the ones coming up the stairs like Armageddon. He whirled at the bestial shout, took a half dozen steps to the door, then stopped, horrified by the sounds coming from beyond the thin boards.

The wall beside his door crumpled, bulged from some heavy impact. The floor shook, once, twice. Paint brushes clattered to the floor, the tin rolling until it hit the bed post.

Goren's bellows twisted an octave higher, turned frantic. Beneath the screams, Tod could hear Robert Geat, his voice a steady murmur in Goren's ear as he pulled him close. Clinching, they rammed against the walls as Goren desperately tried to pull away. A sickening snapping sound echoed along the passage, followed by Goren's scream.

Tod opened the door and stepped into the hall. He saw Goren's fleeing form, plunging down the stairs. Robert Geat stood a dozen feet away, his blue suit spattered with blood. He held Goren's left arm in his hand. The shoulder end rested lightly on the rug, draining into a sodden pool. Crimson drops tapped Tod's shoulder. He stepped back into his doorway, gagging on the stench, streaks of blood and saliva on the battered drywall opposite him.

A woman's scream rose up waveringly from somewhere far below.

Robert Geat nodded. "Abel's vengeance is not yet complete." His heavy gaze swung to Tod. "You're not a poet, but you'll have to do. Remember this, Mr. Coll. I need someone to remember this." He turned and picked something up, then, still carrying Goren's arm, walked past Tod. Halfway to the stairs, he faced Tod one last time. "Here," he tossed an object that Tod instinctively caught. "Keep it. God knows I have to do everything myself around here."

Footsteps thumping down the stairs.

Tod looked down and found a brass cup in his hand.

• • •

BY THE TIME he reached the main floor, Dam Gigi's screams had died away. Tod crouched down at the foot of the stairs and held his head in hands. *Coward. Coward. Coward.*

The storm rattled the building, swept bitter cold draughts

down the halls. Keening voices sang his name, clawed hands clattered against the windows.

He moaned softly, then looked up as a faint sound reached him.

Death stood by the back door, brushing dust from his cloak. His scythe glimmered wetly where it leaned against the cracked wall. After a moment he turned his attention to Tod. "I'll buy you a beer, Mr. Coll. No one asks for what they can see, or can't. Rest assured in many ways you remain blissfully blind."

Tod's voice was a croak. "That's a comfort?"

"Come. You and I, we'll hold the storm back a while longer." He drifted to Tod's side and looked down on him. "I've had a hell of a night, too."

"I just bet." His bones aching with deep, ineffable needs, Tod slowly climbed to his feet.

Inside Stalker's, Gil had his latest girl on his arm. He spoke quietly in her ear as he led her to the alley door. Other girls stood at the counter, laughing and whispering and watching with menacing intensity.

"What now?" Tod breathed as he sat down at a table. Death sat across from him and beckoned toward the bar.

"Not your average ale," Death said.

His eyes blurring with exhaustion, Tod watched a gaunt spectre approach their table. It set down two dusty bottles, then sank beneath the floorboards.

"The bottles are intrusive, I know," said Death, pulling their corks. "From the siege of Vienna. I was quite taken by a book once . . . . "

A shout erupted from the alley door. They turned to see Gil pushing the young girl into the Kid's arms. The hairy man held her a moment, as if unsure of what to do. Gil laughed, making an obscene gesture. The prostitute wrapped her arms around the Kid and leaned against him. The Kid backed away into the shadows. A dog yowled mournfully.

Gil closed the door and whirled triumphantly. People cheered, a chorus of jaded envy. Oblivious to the nasty, blood-hungry tone, Gil took a bow, then sauntered back to his throne.

Death handed one of the bottles to Tod, who drank mechanically.

"One finds peace in the strangest things," Death said, "the strangest moments in time. Gil's stepped on his road, as yet unaware of it. The Kid's wounding is but moments away. And Robert Geat's about to meet his match."

Tod's head snapped up.

Death nodded, then raised his bottle. "Tonight, Tod Coll, I offer you surcease."

"What I need is inspiration." He took another mouthful.

"Patience," Death murmured. "When it comes, the waiting will end. That's all, Tod Coll. When it comes."

A fine haze, warm and calming, swept through Tod. He studied the bottle in his hands, its scratched, pitted surface, the maker's stamp, and only now realised what he'd put into his body. For this night, he knew, he'd be blind.

CHAPTER SIX

He took the Skytrain west, out over the ocean's choppy waves, waves like hammered copper in the early light. He'd awakened, tucked into his bed with no memory of how he got there. Rested, remnants of peace drifting through him.

The hallway had been scrubbed clean, the walls so well repaired there was no sign of the damage from the night before.

He'd walked deserted, dark streets to the terminal, pleased with the solitude.

By the time he stepped into the Skytrain, the calm had begun to waver, tremors of desperation making him edgy, eager for the rising sun. The storm had drifted south of the bay, but from out here he could see it swinging back, moving in on the city, the cloud-wreathed woman impossibly tall, seeming to hunch beneath the roof of stars.

He was running out of time, lost out here over the endless waves. Fleeing from, fleeing to, maybe.

Into the shadow of Town Lincolns and loud opinions, or

the quick swoop into fame's tumbling stream, cape streaming and suit glistening like a Spandex condom. Some squares on the canvas and a diagonal slash of dull paint, a hundred grand at the New York auction thanks very much. As much substance as the head of a beer, but what the hell, goes down easy, right?

An island appeared ahead, a small green lump on the copper seas.

The Skytrain made a course correction, headed for it in a swift descent. Tod saw buildings on it now, blinding white domes, pillars, a grove of cedars. Robed figures wandering the grounds. The Skytrain slowed, slid into a landing.

The doors hissed open and Tod stepped out onto tiled marble. The main building stood off to the right, at the end of a pathway lined in mistletoe. On the clipped lawn to the left was a sign that read *Oak Grove Retirement Complex*.

He headed into the building and found the reception desk. A large muscular woman sat behind it, working a calculator and making notes. Vipers writhed from her head, all turning to eye Tod as he approached.

One of the snakes spoke, "Can I help you?" A tongue flicked out expectantly.

"I need inspiration," Tod said. Numbness deadened his limbs, thickened his tongue. "When it comes, the waiting will end. That's all."

Another snake answered, "Down the hall, third door on the left."

The woman hadn't looked up yet, still calculating, still jotting notes.

"That's handy," Tod said. He pushed himself forward, his steps woodenly taking him down the hall to the third door on the left. He opened it and walked in.

A large sunny room, French doors opened to a courtyard,

a single enormous bed—maybe a hundred fifty square feet— with a pillow the size of a mattress. Oak and laurel leaves scattered over the floor, dry and crunching underfoot as Tod headed for the French doors. No paintings, no other furnishings, zinc white walls, zinc white bed sheets, zinc white tiles under the leaves.

He heard voices in the courtyard, the trickle of a fountain. He stepped outside, into the harsh sunlight. Curved stone benches encircled the fountain, crowded with old women in white robes. Others sat by the water's edge, making wicker baskets. Beyond the courtyard stood a grove of oaks, planted in a circle around a flat-topped boulder. More old women wandered among the trees.

Tod felt a strange certainty lodge inside him—they were sisters. All of them, sisters. He heard their voices filling his head, but none of them were talking, wrinkled lips pressed into tight, stitched lines. Words and images poured through him, wave after wave.

> *Promises rent from every sapling, every beast that walked that crawled that swam the rivers and lakes and seas every beast that eyed the constellations and found us that ploughed the earth and found us that speared his side and found us that flew high in ethereal fancy and found us. Promises rent and loved by all—*
> *—weeping at dogwood's roots, the childslayer—*
> *—should the thorns prick you wash thoroughly apply antiseptic*
> *(the thorns prick*
> *prick you*
> *you wash*
> *wash thoroughly*
> *thoroughly apply*

apply antiseptic, well what do you know?)
  and use a sterile bandage. Or bind with plantain what
the hell those old ladies knew their stuff—
  —that clapped their hands in the deep recesses
thundering like hooves and found us that piled the skulls
and hid the tattoos on lower back with bihedral flanged
adzes to ply the secret knowledge in every valley and found
us that hid their temples in the grottos forgotten by the cars
overhead and found us that walked the world's deserts
spoke to no one until the beast came with warmth and the
promise of wounding and found us—
  —into this new wise age of
post-modern-paternal-regard-for-the-Third-World-poor-saps-
sorry-we-stepped-on-you-here's-a-cool-million-and-a-Fanta-
factory-where's-the-beef-pc-pseudo-intellectual-neo-puritanism
-what-the-hell's-wrong-with-my-English-you-fucking-fascist-
we-bought-shares-in-macblo-pre-post-neo-romantic-revisionism
-get-out-of-my-sweat-lodge-you-pale-pink-animated-moan—
  —and all the children sang their death-cries in the toxic
ferment of his tyranny—
  —the gargoyle is symbolic of male oppression and
objectification with the blindfold representing the implicit
male desire for anonymity in expressing power and the
scales suggesting a need to redress the balance of genders,
too bad about all that white paint—
  —that walked in the language of dreams and found us
that creamed the centrefold and found us promises rent in
the secret places to fend the ones who can see who never
found us who'll never find us because she comes in the
storm of chaos we're the sisters of your inspiration Tod Coll
and we're nothing but lies—
  —because our society has forgotten reciprocity, not only
on the macro-social scale, but also on the micro-social (the

individual, if you will) scale of human interaction. While talent may be deemed a gift it nevertheless is not free and the struggles of Tod Coll may be viewed as the macro-society's expression of reciprocal punishment. Like any large non-homogenous organism displaying homogenous traits of collective behaviour, society prefers not to see, recognition being a kind of education and education being a call to arms and a call to arms being bloody, messy and confusing, frightening—

—and the frog in the pot on the stove who found us but too fucking late—

—promises of the free easy ride mind the mistletoe Tod Coll but now you have it, gratis, tax-free all the inspiration you can gush out with pot after pot of strong tea ignore the bloated amphibian in the kettle and let's piss out a storm to wow the world and make worshippers of vampires and dinner-guests of cannibals . . .

Book Three

Who Can See

CHAPTER SEVEN

He sat on the bench, wondering where the old men had gone. The pond was full of ducks, so crowded in there all he saw was their heads rising up from what looked like a single, massive body. An avian wave, surging randomly, moved by hidden tidal forces. Some heads, near the leading edges of the wave, disappeared under the water, never to reappear.

He felt loose, relaxed, ready to paint. Images filled his head, more images than he could imagine existed. He still had an hour before his meeting with Stephen Tyme and Bernard. The morning sky was gray, smelling of rain. The same out over the harbour. The storm was gone.

Finding this bench empty—his friends nowhere in sight— troubled him, a small, unsettling kind of trouble. He wanted to talk with them, wanted to share his revelation, his gift of inspiration, he wanted them to know that faith was worth keeping—he wanted to see George smile in answer to that.

The ducks rose in a frantic chorus. Something was happening out in the middle of the pond. Water foamed into a bulge, sending the birds tumbling. A duck caught on the surge flapped its wings, rose quickly—but not quick enough. From the water a sword flashed, skewering the duck as it slashed upward. The woman's hand gripping the slimy hilt was white, pale as bone.

The duck slowly slid down to the hilt, leaving a red stain in its wake. Its head dangled against the woman's hand. The sword poised there for a long moment, then sank downward, taking the bird with it.

A pond full of ducks, surging with unseen tidal forces, one body, a thousand heads. From over the harbour came the rumble of thunder.

• • •

TOD HURRIED DOWN the street, the wind whipping after him. From between his lips ran a steady torrent of curses, the voice pushing people out of his way, giving him a straight, vicious line.

He crossed an intersection against the traffic, snarled at the screeching cars. Rain spat at his back, pellets of con-tempt—*kill the children*—the wild songs filling the air with his name.

He had a meeting. He had his inspiration, his ideas, his images, the itch in his hands. Fuck the storm, too late the storm, too late the lady's embrace and the clack of bangles that might be shackles. He had the Gallery of Art between his legs, a closet for Narcisse, a wooden stake for Mr. San-guire. He had his meeting. Ten a.m. sharp and the itch in his hands.

He stalked onward, crossing another intersection, coming upon St. Michael's with its brocaded steps and stiff doors, its robes on the altar and its kisses on the knuckles, neo-post-pastoral-paternalism and three little men in a limo.

Parked in the loading zone in front of St. Michael's steps, in vulgar architecture of pitched timbers and five tin-pitted iron gears, stood an instrument of the Inquisition. Graffiti scarred the beams—*Isabella was here Expel the Gypsies the Jews the athletes from the People's Republic of China This rack goes a long way*—

Tod jerked to a stop, seeing the figure spread-eagled on its bed. He wiped, then clawed his eyes. Lightning flashed behind him, thunder rolling like boulders down a hill.

Johan's head turned. His eyes had been carved from their sockets, his face pocked with burns. His scabbed lips smiled. "Should've heard my sermon," he said softly. "Art and ethics, Tod. I called it *No Fucking in the Foyer*." He paused. "I call this one *Who Can See*. You're the first person who's noticed me, and they were hoping for a public display."

"They're out of touch," Tod said. "No emcee."

"No jaycee."

Tod wiped his face, took a deep breath. "Stop this, Johan. Stop the storm. I'm ready for the Gallery of Art, I'm ready for comfort—I know what to do with it, I won't forget, Johan."

Johan shook his head. "Can't stop the storm, Tod."

Tod's fist hammered the timber, then he slumped against the machine, head bowed.

"I can slow it," Johan said.

Tod's head snapped up.

"Just one night, Tod. Is that what you want?"

"One night. Tonight. You can give me tonight?"

"Is that what you're asking me to do?"

"Can you do it, Johan?"

"Are you asking me to?"

"Yes!"

The fingers of Johan's right hand twitched. "Okay, Tod. I'll hold on. Get going, then. You're late for your appointment."

The wind died, a few last gusts, the songs fading away, drawing back to the harbour. Tod pushed himself from the instrument, wheeled and half-ran down the street.

I'll hold on. What did Johan mean by that?

•   •   •

BUCKETS OF MONEY a drop of blood the people's radio station live and taped they promise they won't ask about the mistletoe *what about that mistletoe, Mr. Coll?* into the scene and the pallid leeches on your tail *for whom does the swan come in white panoply, Mr. Coll?* the Sun the Prov the Cow over the Moon the timely colonists with their double-deckers and hanging pots fertilised with Babylon's ashes into the scene with eccentric quirks, strangeness and charm *it's fucking Magnum .44 Tod my boy* there's a peasant crusade in the foyer, Mr. Mayor *thanks, Sue, kick in the balls, right, Tod?* Andre Narcisse on line 2, Mr. Mayor *thanks, Sue, take a message you feeling inspired, Tod boyo Sky's the limit who the fuck said that I'll eat him alive you feeling inspired?* I'm feeling inspired. *You feeling inspired, Tod?* I'm feeling inspired. *You feeling inspired, Mistletoed boyo?*

Like a swan, gentlemen, like a swan.

•   •   •

HIGH ON THE MOUNT, God spoke through Tod's brush. Wet style, no time for anything else, canvas after canvas on the sacred assembly line. His room a museum to the modern, before it's modern. Tubes disgorging worms of custom mix—lemon yellow, peach orange, banana green, cherry red, unripe crab-apple ochre, grape purple, grape green, pips brown, orange orange, grapefruit yellow, grapefruit pink, mango red, kumquat chartreuse, breadfruit brown, mana magenta.

A garden of colours, a bounty of gifts spilling into images. His room a temple, his desk an altar, his brush a knife. Plucking ribs, tossing snakes, burning witches, sewing cervixes, drowning down wells, measuring ladles of guilt, suppressing, oppressing, slamming the doors, cursing the blood, walking on the moon, probing satellites into Venusian mysteries, burying her chaos in the clutter of tomes, binding her arms, binding her feet, run from the tottering broad, chick, babe, ho' bitch slut virgin, run from the unknown call it unknowable call out to the blood of kings and the angry young men and let's kill in righteousness and fear.

The storm circled the city, faint songs and thunder. Johan's gift, the heaving black clouds came no closer. Hours passed, measured in the Skytrain's circling regard, and the sacrifices continued.

Silence from the hall, silence from Goren's old room. Down below Gil and the Kid wrestled in Stalker's Bar, smashing tables in their muscle on muscle clinches. Crowds cheered. It'd been going on all night, without pause, without rest.

Tod painted, killing canvases, gutting tubes of custom mix. Every brush stroke pushed her away. He was vague on who she was, but it didn't seem to matter. The woman in the storm, Lady Justice, the mistress from the pond, Athenia Crane. All the same, now. With their blindfold knots kept tight, their empty portfolios of the court-rooms, tomes and swords and skewered ducks. All the same, all trapped in the circling Skytrain. Every brush stroke pushed them away. It was sweet, it was lovely.

Another painting, a last death throe. Tod moved it aside and reached for a new canvas. He dropped it on the desktop, then froze.

The gargoyle and Lady Justice—he'd forgotten to finish the calcining. Too much of the scene exposed, the faces all too clear, the dear lady and the leering gargoyle's lust-twisted visage—now turning to him, now smiling. On the canvas the shadow of his own head was nowhere to be seen, just the gargoyle's face—his own face.

CHAPTER EIGHT

He stumbled in the street, down to his hands and knees, his breaths coming in gasps. The Skytrain hissed by overhead.

He'd done what they'd asked. He'd taken the gifts, the money, the inspiration, the time. A short nudge, then, to find his own private monster, the one inspired by hatred. A short nudge, from fear into hatred. Fear into hatred.

The storm rumbled. Time was running out. *I'll hold on—* God, what did Johan mean? *Is that what you want? Is that what you want? Is that what you want?* Thrice the question, once the answer.

Are you inspired, boyo?

Tod lurched to his feet, began running. Blocks jolting past, street corners, blinking red lights, buildings. He wheeled around a corner and staggered into the square. His steps slowed.

The gargoyles were down from their pillars. One held her legs pinned on the dusty sidewalk, pressing down with taloned hands on her bare, bloodied ankles. The other fucked her, pausing after every thrust for a punch to her face.

The scales were in the gutter puddle. Tod ran forward and grasped the chain, then turned to the scene at the foot of the pedestal. He shouted as he attacked, one step closer and a wild swing at the gargoyle at her feet. It looked up in time to see the heavy brass plate slam into its face. Bone crunched, the gargoyle's head snapped back with a loud crack before the creature fell back to the sidewalk.

A bony hand punched Tod in the side of his head. He reeled back, dropping the scales and raising his hands before his face. The gargoyle picked him up and threw him to the pavement.

Tod gagged, unable to breathe as pain lanced through his chest.

The gargoyle knelt over him and started beating—face, head, stomach, chest, arms—methodically. Through bleeding ears, Tod heard its soft laughter. He realised he was going to die. Punches loosed whimpers from his throat. He was going to die, then the gargoyle would finish with her— the same thing, ceaseless fists driving home.

Tod twisted desperately, shot an arm forward, hand closing on the gargoyle's scrotum. He squeezed as hard as he could. A faint crunch, drowned out by the gargoyle's screaming. Get 'em where they live. The creature rolled to one side, curling up into a ball. Tod wiped blood from his eyes, dragged himself away. His groping hand found chains. The scales. He pulled them close, twisted a length of the chain around his fists, then lifted his head, searching for the gargoyle.

It hadn't moved, save for a slow rocking, its screams diminished to a whimper.

Tod crawled to its side, forced the chain around its throat, and began pulling, rhythmically sawing the chain back and forth. The gargoyle thrashed, but Tod leaned back out of reach, pulling steadily, sawing rhythmically. Blood made the chain slippery—he dug his nails into his palms for a better grip.

The front of the gargoyle's head came away, hinged by vertebrae, a crimson tide sweeping down the front of its chest. It had stopped moving. Hadn't moved for some time, he realised. Tod loosened the chain, fumbled to free his hands from the links, then crawled to the pedestal. He sat up, leaned back against the cool stone.

Are you inspired, boyo?

Twisting his head, he looked up over his shoulder. She was back, looming over him, tomes in the crook of her right arm, left arm raised with the scales hanging motionless. One of the plates was dented.

After a few minutes, Tod pulled himself upright. He swung his gaze to Justice Hall, then started up the steps.

The glass doors opened to him. He walked inside, turning left, into the Office of the Mayor. No one at reception, of course. No one anywhere at all. Tod walked to Sue's office. As he entered he saw faint light bleeding out from under Stephen's door, heard a muttering voice.

"You didn't listen," Stephen was saying. "I warned you."

Tod heard the Mayor licking his fingers, chewing, swallowing. Bone cracking, an inhaling sound as he sucked out the marrow.

Something moaned.

"I said I'd do it, didn't I? Fucking pimple-faced upstart— who the fuck did you think you were dealing with? Too late now, though, isn't it? Here I am." He licked his fingers again. "Doing what I said I'd do, you poor little shit."

Silently, Tod backed out of Sue's office and shut the door.

• • •

THE STORM TOWERED over the city, no lightning, no thunder, just the black, bruised cloud. No wind, no rain. Shapes moved inside it. Dawn was still an hour away.

The doors to the Gallery of Art were open, as Tod knew they would be. Circling, he was circling, making his rounds. Nothing could stop him—he couldn't stop him himself. The deadly path closing in, closing down. Time ticking away.

Narcisse in macro-scale. The giant painting was suspended by chains, spotted by tracklighting, a thick patina of oily dust on the acrylic. Tod stepped around it, moved into the chambers of Andre's brilliance. One room after another, eternally lit, humidity perfected, temperature controlled, the very vapours of life conditioned into something dead, motionless, stale in the lungs.

Into the last room. Into the latest series, said the sign. *Narcisse in the Flesh.* No more condoms, bed-springs, polynesian canoe prows carved into penises. Just acrylic. Acrylic, and something else. Tod stepped closer to the nearest painting. Acrylic, and bits of flesh.

Smooth skin, delicately lacquered. Tufts of hair: facial, scalp, pubic. Pieces of flesh, muscle tissue, fat tissue. Tendons, ligaments, splinters of bone.

In growing horror, Tod walked from one painting to the next, coming to the last one. Alone on the far wall. An ear here, another there. Eyebrows, a glazed eye—Narcisse blue, a new colour—a chin, a cheek. In the centre of it all, surrounded in acrylic, his full-lipped, sensuous mouth.

Tod stood in front of it, staring.

"Are you inspired yet?" the mouth asked.

Narcisse in the Flesh.

•   •   •

PLUCKING DUCKS in the dull early morning light. Feathers danced down the sidewalk on gusts of wind. The pond rippled, its surface like mucous.

"Dear Tod," Rolly said, "you look like hell. Here, take my seat. I've a mind to leave, once and for all, and Devil take the swan."

"I thought I saw her this morning," Sig said. "A glimmer, there in the centre of the pond."

Tod opened his mouth, then closed it again.

"Not enough dead poets," Art said. "Maybe if I keep scaring the children . . . "

Tod said, "Didn't see any of you around last night."

Rolly ran a hand through his wispy hair. "We saw the swan, and gave determined pursuit. Alas, it fled into the storm." He sighed loudly, his eyes drifting to the pond. "George just smiled, of course."

Sig grunted. "I was always convinced the swan was a wild goose chase. Or, rather—"

"I know what you mean, Sig," Tod closed his eyes.

"The storm is returning, it seems—I've a mind to leave."

"Don't," Tod said, climbing to his feet and meeting Rolly's ancient eyes. "Don't leave, Rolly. Hold onto the faith. She's out there, and she's coming."

Rolly's smile was soft. "We know that, Tod," he said quietly.

"When she comes," George said, "the waiting will end. That's all."

•   •   •

JOHAN SACRISTI'S MOUTH parted a crack. "I can feel the sun, Tod."

Tod looked up at the gray, heaving clouds. "It's bright this morning," he said.

Johan nodded. "Warm."

"You shouldn't have done it," Tod said. "You shouldn't have held on for me."

"Inspiration's a delicate thing, friend."

"Narcisse is a work of art."

"Indeed he is."

"No, I mean *he's a work of art.*"

"Ah, well, it had to come to that, eventually, didn't it?"

"Johan, you can let go of the storm now. Please."

"A gift, Tod, freely given without thought of recompense."

Tod jerked forward, leaned over his friend. "*That's* your mistake, Johan! That always been your mistake. Nothing's for free."

"A moral precept . . . "

"Fuck the moral precepts! Your lord did all the suffering so you wouldn't have to—talk about the road to hell being paved! You must've known! That's why you're lying there with your eyes carved out. Sure as the sun rises, your lord earned it—how dare they say it gives the rest of us a free fucking ride?"

"Not free, Tod. We have our guilt, son."

"Yeah," he snapped. "The one that makes you bend over backwards till you crack in two. You can't spend your whole life placating, Johan. That vessel you're pouring your soul into is fucking *bottomless!*"

"A beautiful concept, don't you think? One giant bank vault of a concept. Anyway," he sighed, "the point's academic."

"Not to me it isn't, dammit. I've got to deal with your death. I've got to deal with your suffering, staying alive to hold back the storm. No gifts are free, Johan, can't you see that?"

Johan didn't move, moments passing and he lay still as death. Then he whispered, "Forgive me. I would desire . . . no placating, Tod."

"I've got no choice, friend. But I'll try—I'll try to make it short and sweet."

His friend nodded.

"Let go, now, Johan. It's over."

He watched him die, a few minutes, no longer.

He could hear rush-hour traffic, but the street fronting St. Michael's was empty. Tod stepped back from the instrument, bemusedly looked around. He saw flashing red lights a half block away and headed for them.

Mayor Stephen Tyme was having a parade. Four policemen rested their motorcycles in front of the Mayor's white convertible limo—the one he saved for victories—and the Mayor sat in the back seat, talking with his daughter.

Tod moved closer, waited.

Stephen's polished gaze swept across him, then swept back. "Good God, what the hell happened to you?" He gestured Tod over, shaking his head at two men in business suits who'd been edging up behind Tod.

"I got mugged," he answered, reaching the limo's side. "What's the parade for, Stephen?"

"Sky's dropped," the Mayor replied, chuckling. "Out of the race, into seclusion. Officially, we're celebrating some obscure Japanese holiday—good for business, you know."

Tod glanced upward. "I think you'll get rained on."

"Parade's only going three blocks," Stephen said.

"Oh."

Athenia asked, "How is your painting coming along, Mr. Coll?"

"Just fine. And your portfolio?"

"I've been accepted into law school."

Tod's eyes flicked to Stephen, but the Mayor was busy whispering in his driver's ear.

"Delighted to hear it," Tod said. "Give 'em hell, Ms. Crane."

The smile she turned on her father might have been benign, but Tod doubted it.

Stephen grinned up at Tod. "Care to join us?"

"No. Thought I'd go jogging in the park."

Stephen wasn't listening, his smiled fixed, his eyes scanning the growing crowd. "Time to roll," he said, tapping his driver's shoulder.

The driver honked. The four policemen pulled up their black hoods then kicked their motorcycles into gear.

Tod stepped back into the crowd. Athenia gave him a wave, then the cavalcade was off, Mayor Stephen Tyme waving at blurred faces, the storm clouds rumbling overhead.

● ● ●

DESCENDING, FINALLY DESCENDING, black and billowing. The women raced above the trees, calling to him as he ran down the path. A new path, a different one that would take him to a field of manicured grass.

He'd let them take him there, if he could. If he had the time.

The wind, when it finally came, was like a fist, thrown down through the trees. Branches snapped, ancient firs groaned. Ahead, through stinging eyes, he saw the clearing, under a sky as dark as night.

Tod laughed, the sound tinny to his own ears, and stumbled into the wide, remorseless open. The wind slapped him to the ground. Scraping the mud from his face, he clambered to his feet and plunged forward a few yards more.

The women swept down out of the cloud, whirling around him, reaching out clawed hands as they passed. Faces like white hearts, full crimson lips open to voices cold as the ocean depths. Naked but for long, wind-splayed hair. They darted in close as he staggered on, soft cold hips and thighs brushing against him, claws lightly raking his clothing, voices singing his name and sending it deep inside him, down into the bones then outward again, racing with his blood, echoing in his gasping breath.

He could run no longer. Stopping, turning, painfully straightening.

And she had come. Arms outstretched, bangles racing with red fire, lightning in her black, star-studded hair. Each flash revealing a new face, a skull, something demonic, something angelic, pink-skinned, brown, yellow, black, blue.

The embrace began to close, sweeping down through stars, galaxies, trailing tendrils of chaos. The first set of arms alabaster, the next ebony, seashell pink, mahogany, arms closing and closing.

He felt her touch, and screamed.

Always apart, with his secret pigments and the potions that rock would swallow and never give up. Creature of words, when the words fall away and all that's left for the things crowding the secret spirit world in his skull were his hands. Stains, sweeping black lines spat out of a bone tube, colours of earth, of hide, sweet lines of muscle, a hint of depth mocking these flat walls. Depth was the secret pathway into the spirit world, where all thoughts were born. With depth, the mind exploded, and nothing was ever the same again.

He would lead them into the rock, into the womb whose walls shocked the eye, the mind, whispered of the world beyond. And in the thunder of clapping hands and droning reeds he would give them the souls of the beast.

He would—no, it was wrong. He was a she—

—jarred anything loose yet, you know, racial memories, archetypes?—

—dreaming of betrayal, hunting for that look in his mother's eye, that look in every mother's eye, something that went back beyond kings and beyond borders, and beyond wars and beyond chivalry's two-edged blade. Something that went back, and back. A two-edged story, one hidden in the other, all that romantic revisionism (a word not yet found, just lived, here in these gloomy halls with the barrows of old heroes groomed by sheep), and all the deadly meanings behind the king's betrayal. A story of words awaiting some bald-pated illumination in all diligent ignorance of pagan throes in history's muddled memory. Oh, write on, you unwashed flea-bitten fool, take my ancient echoes so cunningly voiced and metered that the beauty is all you sense, take this bitter poet's memory of the betrayal in his mother's eyes—

—anything? No echoes at all? Oh my, oh my—

—and all the promises rent save the lowly mistletoe sleeping there beneath the rock (fancy that, rock again) that some foolish football player with golden hair and a minimum wage job manning a toll-bridge might walk fearless from his father's pain and his mother's arms smiling at his manifest destinies one smooth easy slide with nothing earned—oops who pricked me with that

*mistletoe and what about that national anthem excusing
me from all harm is that joker who I think it is shit I'm not
feeling too good and vows rent from heroes across the world
into oh into the underworld for that faded old running back
selling cars in Hades in all his myriad uniforms—*

—and they speared his side

—and they speared his side

—and they nailed him to a tree

—nailed him to a tree

*—how many of these blighters are there, anyway,
fuckin' hell—*

*—oh, come on, Tod, I'm the little bird at your shoulder
who told you and showed you and pricked you and
answered the echoes of everything you'd thought you'd
never seen before, heard before, tasted before, touched
before. Subcontextual metafictional charades didn't cha
know didnchano dijnano deja vu how far back do you
need, Tod, let's try one more one more—*

*—A dragon coiled around him, its scales seeming to roll
like marbles against his naked flesh. Muscles contracted,
pulling him down. He felt cold, wet clay sliding under him,
then water.*

*The sun burned hot overhead, a searing flash in his eyes
as the dragon twisted him around. The edges of a watering
hole, savanna grasses, distant dusty hills, all crazily tilting.
Sliding down, into the water. He tried to scream again, the
sound coming out like a bleat. Muscles immediately
tightened a fraction more around his chest.*

*Tod felt his ribs crack. A single coil rose up under his
chin. He jerked his head and sank his canines into the cold,
salty flesh. The coil flinched. He bit again, twisting with
his left arm, into the second flinching, between two coils.
Free, his arm reaching back to the clay—an arm covered in*

reddish hair, torn away in patches, stained with mud. He sank his blunt fingers into the bank.

The dragon's head appeared, its black tongue flickering out, then in.

The head flashed forward in a blur. He felt it impact his skull, the coils around his body loosening as the serpent surged forward. Fire lit Tod's brain. Uncoiling, sliding in, sliding inside wrapping around his spinal cord. The pressure released, gone. Freed.

Tod rolled over, covered in wet clay already hardening under the hot African sun.

A voice spoke inside him: What I would fashion, it said, you could not guess—

—give it over, cousin, it's time for the man to forget remembrance and start thinking, so I stayed at the gate and let cousin hop after you, I'm always staying at the gate, outside the motel door, at the bathroom dispenser, in the bed beside your sleeping wife, but you come around you always come around—

—thoroughly apply antiseptic in all matters of mystery so the revolution establishes our clean zinc white dominance in segments in chapters in factors in charts in point form in bits in test-tubes in diagrams in maps in eras in periods in ages in fractions in quotients in laws in sentences in paragraphs in glottal stops in upwardly mobile neo-Marxist evolutionary climbers into the clean bright world where we can treat everything if we get to it soon enough meaning recognising the signs is everything and kill those fucking poets who needs mystery and wonder when you've got Nintendo and circuit board daycare and three-act adaptations with all the knots closing in perfect silk executive board unison and who needs painters when you've got digitalized virtual reality and plug-in

*imaginations divisible by threes and subsidiary rights and
black-winged spiked-tail national debt a buzz-saw barking
the trees of life and get a fucking real job you snot-nosed
little boygirlboygirl we know what's work it's work which is
work that which is work is work is work and it must mean
something because ethic comes after it and the stocks are
soaring into ursine and ungulate constellations of bright
lights surrounded by a whole lot of nothing but man I'm
dreaming about eight thousand different styles of
automotive transportation and you take that away from me
you've got fuckin' trouble—*

*—thinkable thoughts wouldn't you say, Tod, and what
face would you put on it, I mean, is this the dragon's
thoughts, and would that be roots of emotion he's gnawing
at, or is it the other way and who really cares?—*

*—I've got Michelangelo's head in a mason jar, wait till
you see the clones, wait till you see the fucking billboards!
Selling God was a cakewalk back then, wasn't it, I've got
neo-puritans in my stable, man, gotta find the easy kind of
indignation, that doesn't cost a fuckin' cent drop of sweat
or micron of inconvenience I've got central park joggers .9
CO clamouring for slash-through-cigarette tables by the
window working their bodies like medieval peasants wore
out at forty hooked on natural morphine it's right there in
your head just some agony getting to it no meat please I'll
take that lettuce that only cost thirty-two avian amphibian
invertebrate subspecies species family class phylum in that
useless swampland other side of the river and if I hear that
one dolphin died for that lettuce you're in a whole lot of
trouble where's that drunk with the Fiat keys think he's
going get him a taxi to take him home so he can beat up
his wife and kids so long as the curtains are closed and the
front lawn is cut with regularity and the purple loosestrife's*

*in bloom god I love nuclear families who turned out the
lights where's my lettuce I can't eat what I can't see—*

*—there, that's better isn't it, Tod, too much going on all
around you to waste time living past lives (unless you can
squeeze a bestseller out of it) but I suppose you're like the
rest. Rather not think, rather not think at all, who knows
what might show up and direct your hand. That's where I
come in, sweeping in on Kali's absolute gifts that cost
everything but you must know it's worth it and let's face it
she's coming for us all thank heavens. No accident the
politicians fear chaos, you know. Order underneath keeps
the tower stable, keep all those shoulders to an occasional
passive shrug, but do you think the anger's building, Tod?
Do you really think so? Do you really think?*

*So comes the final question, but moments before she
sweeps through and past and out of and maybe into.
Comes the final question, Tod. Whatever will you paint
now?*

THE EMBRACE passed through him, a woman's touch of
destruction and rebirth. Songs drifted around him, hungry
for some distant war. He sensed her presence, a warm smell
of blood, something bemused, something frowning,
something searching for words.

Tod found he could speak. "Inspired by fear," he said.
"Inspired by hatred. I'd like something else."

A voice all around. "I hear you, but what you are, I could
not guess."

"I can see."

"I can't."

The frown—unseen only felt—deepened.

Tod groped for something to say, but she spoke first.

"Show me."

● ● ●

GIL AND THE KID, the Kid bruised and bloody, sharing a joke over their glasses of port.

Tod wiped the mud from his face. All the girls were there, except for one. He saw Death at the counter, walked over.

"I took her last night," Death said.

"Oh, but she was so young."

Death gestured at one of the brown bottles in front of him. "I've been waiting for you, Mr. Coll."

Tod took the bottle. "The fatal sip, then?"

"No, that's a while yet."

He drank down a sweet mouthful, then leaned on the railing. "She was so young."

"No life for a girl. She's for the Kid. I'll come for him soon."

"I've got a whole bunch of paintings to get rid of—shame about the canvases and frames, though."

"Shall I wipe the slates clean?"

"Can you do that?"

"I do it all the time."

"Thanks."

"Don't mention it."

● ● ●

HE TOOK THE BOTTLE with him to his room. And the pocket book Death gave him. Something about the siege of Vienna. Atrocious cover, but what the hell, he tossed it on the bed.

A white canvas waited on the desk-top. Tod sat down.

"All right," he said. "Johan Sacristi's death, a gift repaid, short and sweet. Called *Who Can See*. I'll show you."

Alizarin crimson, the blood of martyrs. just a hint of a smear, there, between his ribs and against the folds of ebony robe.

Voices on a radio in the room above him, voices drifting down. Glib banter like crows on a hanging tree, the discussion flowing seamless into a tragic suicide, a John Doe who'd stepped into the Skytrain's path on its twilight run. A terrible mess. A lone witness seeing it all close-up, her portfolio spattered with gore . . .

And now for this.

Tragic cycles as certain as sunset, Peace in madness, a rightful claim to the returning voices to paint afresh the hosed-down world.

He heard steps on the stairs. The thump of heels on the landing, heels being dragged down the hall. Keys jangling.

Tod smiled. *Goren's back.*

A Note on the 3-Day Novel-Writing Contest

The **Anvil Press International 3-Day Novel Contest** (formerly sponsored by Pulp Press), the world's most infamous literary marathon, takes place during the Labour Day weekend (the weekend of the first Monday in September) on typewriters and word processors around the world. As the new sponsors of this uniquely Canadian phenomenon, we are thoroughly convinced of the contest's value and importance to writers of long fiction, and remain confident that future contests will discover other fine talents waiting for a suitable challenge.

The rules are simple: entrants, having filled out a registration form and paid the entry fee, begin writing at 12:01 a.m. Saturday, and must stop at or before 12 midnight Monday. The novels may be written in any location and using whatever method, so long as the writing takes place during the three prescribed days. If you cannot type, or do not have access to a typewriter or computer, you are permitted to have your handwritten novel typed during the week following the contest. Entrants then return their finished novels (except handwritten manuscripts) to Anvil Press sometime during the week following the contest, accompanied by a self-addressed stamped envelope and a statement by a witness confirming the novel's completion over the Labour Day Weekend. The winner is announced October 31.

First prize is publication and instant notoriety.

For registration forms and/or more information, send a self-addressed stamped envelope (or $1.00 if outside Canada, as non-Canadian stamps are not useable) to:

> *3-Day Novel Contest*
> *Anvil Press Publishers*
> *#204-A – 175 East Broadway*
> *Vancouver, B.C. CANADA V5T 1W2*
> *PH: (604) 876-8710 FAX: (604) 879-2667*

Write for a free catalogue of other Anvil Press books and pamphlets!

A Note on the 3-Day Novel-Writing Contest

The **Anvil Press International 3-Day Novel Contest** (formerly sponsored by Pulp Press), the world's most infamous literary marathon, takes place during the Labour Day weekend (the weekend of the first Monday in September) on typewriters and word processors around the world. As the new sponsors of this uniquely Canadian phenomenon, we are thoroughly convinced of the contest's value and importance to writers of long fiction, and remain confident that future contests will discover other fine talents waiting for a suitable challenge.

The rules are simple: entrants, having filled out a registration form and paid the entry fee, begin writing at 12:01 a.m. Saturday, and must stop at or before 12 midnight Monday. The novels may be written in any location and using whatever method, so long as the writing takes place during the three prescribed days. If you cannot type, or do not have access to a typewriter or computer, you are permitted to have your handwritten novel typed during the week following the contest. Entrants then return their finished novels (except handwritten manuscripts) to Anvil Press sometime during the week following the contest, accompanied by a self-addressed stamped envelope and a statement by a witness confirming the novel's completion over the Labour Day Weekend. The winner is announced October 31.

First prize is publication and instant notoriety.

For registration forms and/or more information, send a self-addressed stamped envelope (or $1.00 if outside Canada, as non-Canadian stamps are not useable) to:

3-Day Novel Contest
Anvil Press Publishers
#204-A – 175 East Broadway
Vancouver, B.C. CANADA V5T 1W2
PH: (604) 876-8710 FAX: (604) 879-2667

Write for a free catalogue of other Anvil Press books and pamphlets!

*Co-Winner of the 16th
Annual International
3-Day Novel Writing
Contest . . .*

VACANT ROOMS

by

MITCH PARRY

Copyright © 1994 Mitch Parry

Published by Anvil Press
Suite 204-A 175 East Broadway
Vancouver, B.C., CANADA
V5T 1W2

CANADIAN CATALOGUING IN PUBLICATION DATA

Lundin, Steve.
Stolen voices/Steve Lundin.   Vacant rooms/Mitch Parry

ISBN: 1-895636-06-X

I. Parry, Mitch, 1960- Vacant Rooms. II. Title. III. Title: Vacant
rooms.

PS8573.U543S7 1994   C813'.54   C94-910089-7
PR9199.3.L86S7 1994

Typesetting: Anvil Press

Cover Design: Greg White Illustration & Design

Flip this book over for a second 3-Day Novel.

For Rosana, with love and thanks.

And for Bronwen, who should still be here.

*The mortar which holds the improvised "home"
together—even for a child—is memory.*
— JOHN BERGER

*I think maybe you never get over anything, you just
find a way of carrying it as gently as possible.*
— BRONWEN WALLACE

A picture. Somewhere I have a picture of my mother. A black and white photograph, thirty years old.

My mother outlined in grains of silver. Noon and mid-summer, so she is wearing a wide-brimmed straw hat. A white blouse with lightly coloured flowers and a wide collar. She is standing in the backyard, her pale thin neck matching perfectly the slight curve of the rosebush growing beside her. My father had planted the roses earlier that year; two years later the supposedly perennial plant more or less died from neglect. But in the photo the roses (Queen Elizabeths, I think they're called) are young and full of hope.

Noon and mid-summer: the hat is tied under her chin with a thin leather string. Around the brim of the hat is a bright ribbon, the short tail of which flaps behind her head in the July breeze. In a colour photo the ribbon would probably appear to be bright red, but in this picture it is a band of dark grey, so that is how I will always remember it. Dark grey and frozen in a breeze that once circled a house in southern Ontario before racing itself into stillness.

Because it is noon the hat casts a shadow deep over her face, tiny patches of light escape through the straw weave and shine on her nose and cheeks like a veil. Only her mouth and high cheek bones are clearly visible, a pale v squeezed taut by a staged smile:

say cheese. I imagine that under the shadow is a pair of cat's eye sunglasses providing further protection from the sun which has already reduced her face to a splotchy mask.

Behind my mother's left shoulder are the concrete steps leading to the front door of our home. My father built those steps shortly after he and my mother bought the house. He was always proud of those steps, the hedge he planted around the front lawn, the wooden fence he built to seal off the back yard.

My father, in the middle ground, is visible leaning back, resting against the top two steps. He's looking off into the next yard with his back to the camera. In spite of the brightness of the sun the photo's depth of field is very shallow—Dad's a blur, little more than a thick rug folded up on the steps.

Far away in the background, so small and out of focus that it looks like part of the hedge or another rosebush, is the figure of a five-year-old boy, standing with his legs apart. In one hand he is holding what could be a toy spade, but it could also be a cane or even a golf club; the other hand is raised almost in a salute, shielding his eyes from the sun. If this part of the photo were to be enlarged so that only the boy was visible, where you might expect to find a face there would be nothing more than a smudge of black and grey tatters on a white field.

The photo is bordered in white with the date stamped on the bottom: July 22, 1963. It is edged in perforations which are meant to suggest lace but which only serve to create the impression that this is a large, stiff postage stamp. My mother the Queen, smiling diplomatically, flanked by guards or servants; my father and I a throw-rug, a floor-lamp, in the palace.

Or a stage with a tattered curtain. A woman in a straw hat enters and advances to the foot of the stage where, peering into the darkness of her audience, she delivers the prologue. Her pinched face and trembling voice betray her fear. Behind her a man and a boy interrupt the scenery—a diagonal line, a vertical.

I know that no one is going to meet me at the airport, but when I finally get through customs I still end up looking around for whoever it is I don't expect to be there. I'm still dazed by the flight, new accents, the recent past. I wander the airport for half an hour, afraid of making the decision to continue and not even sure of how to go about doing it. Grandma's instructions were cruelly vague: Catch the coach to Bolton, then take the bus to Horwich.

I finally find the information desk, and have to ask directions twice. It's been nearly twenty years since I last heard this accent close up. Mum managed to bury every trace of Manchester from her own voice, refused even to do parodies at parties while Dad was still alive. By the time I figure out the directions the woman behind the counter has given me, I've already missed the coach to Bolton and have to wait another half hour. But I'm not in a hurry.

Once on the coach I fall into a half-sleep and dream that each breath is a bubble, rising slowly from the bottom of the ocean and breaking long before it reaches the surface.

In Horwich my mother's brother-in-law meets me in front of a news agent's, as arranged. He shakes my hand gently, says he hopes the flight was comfortable. An awkward pause. He tries to

tell me how sorry he is etc. I thank him, and then in unison we shrug our shoulders: *What can one do?*

We are both relieved to have dealt with the formalities.

During the drive to my Grandmother's house Uncle Bill tells me about his new business: he is now an independent lorry-driver. Or, at least, he will be completely self-employed once he has paid off the rest of the money owing on his truck and so on. At some point the drone of his voice must have lulled me back into sleep, because I start and find that the car has stopped in front of a row of old houses. Uncle Bill is looking at me. *Is this the place?*

Grandma is standing in the doorway, looking more or less the same as she did when I last saw her twenty-seven years ago. Her arms are opened, her eyes are closed. We hug in a cloud of musk and baby powder as Uncle Bill carries in my suitcase. He treats it as though it contains a sacred icon from Atlantis.

My grandmother can tell that I am exhausted from the way my embrace folds like a wet rag. She hobbles up the stairs and leads me to my room, tells me to catch up on my sleep. Glances at my luggage. *You need to get some rest.*

The metal frame is so twisted and burned that I can't even guess what make of car it was they had been driving. My father is still strapped to the passenger seat, his back rigid and his

eyes blank as oysters. I pull him from the wreckage and lead him to a bench under a tree. Although he can walk, I know that he is so dazed that he cannot think or feel. I know, too, that he has always been this way, that he can never be any different.

Under the tree I find a canteen full of sweet water. I put it to his mouth, but he doesn't swallow and the water flows out onto his shirt. His eyes flash wide and he begins to flounder, his arms flapping against my chest.

"But we can't leave yet! Not without your mother!"

In the distance there is a faint shimmering, like a mirage on the horizon. I can almost see the outline of a woman crouching in an alleyway; there is the faint sound of sobbing, a glass vase breaking. In my arms my father moans, softly at first, and then louder as he realizes he has lost her.

I wake from the dream pinned down beneath layers of blankets and sheets. The room is dark and damp, the air close. I get out of bed, put on my clothes and stumble to the bathroom, where I splash my face with cold water. My grandmother hears me, calls.

"Dennis, come downstairs and have something to eat."

I obey because there is nothing else to do. Halfway down the stairs she calls again, this time less confidently.

"Perhaps you should bring . . . "

I go back to my room and open the larger of my two suitcases. I can hear the sound of a kettle whistling from the kitchen below.

Like a brass vase, really, capped and slightly less tarnished than the ones that line my grandmother's windowsills. Fairly small, and surprisingly unobtrusive, although right now it looms over Grandma and me like a derelict tower. She points, waves her hand in the direction of the unspeakable.

"I suppose that's . . . ?"

The tea scalds the roof of my mouth, already shredded from the marmalade and toast, but I do not flinch. I swallow, place my cup back on its saucer. My late breakfast.

"Yes, it is. Was. Well, still is, I guess."

Grandma purses her lips, sucks her tea gently. Sniffs. Her eyes are watery and red behind her glasses.

"I see."

We sip silently. Through the window I can see that the sun is setting in a limp blaze of muted orange. In the kitchen the light is already beginning to grow thin.

I remember flannel sheets orange and warm as tangerines.

I remember flannel sheets orange and warm as tangerines. My mother snaps them out and fills the air with the smell of fresh laundry and a breeze rich with pollen. She snaps the sheets again before spreading them out on the bed, slips the pillows into bright orange pillowcases. She laughs, tosses the pillows onto the bed like sacks of summer light.

She sings:

She's a lassie from Lan-ca-sheer

and laughs again.

I am standing beside the wardrobe my father had ordered from England, where my Grandma and Grandpa live. My mother waves to me, smiles. There are lace curtains in the bedroom window; they flap in the breeze like slow flags, like the orange sheets. She calls me My Love, tells me it's time to go to bed. Through the window I can see my father sitting on the front steps, reading the paper in the warm evening air.

I am five years old; I have my whole life ahead of me.

After tea Uncle Bill drops by and asks if I want to go down to the local for a pint. A quick glance at my grandmother—she doesn't want to come with us.

We walk beneath sulphur-yellow street lamps, around the corner to the Grapes. Inside, the pub is warmly lit and noisy. A young man is playing a slot machine by the door. Uncle Bill leads me to the bar, orders a pint of stout and asks me what I want.

"A pint of bitter." Because I have always loved the way it sounds. But the beer arrives chilled. "I thought English beer was served warm?"

"No longer," he says. "Everything's changed now. Country's nothing like what it was. No jobs, no money. Tradition's dying. Not like last time you were over here. I blame it on immigration—refugees, you know."

He catches my eye, testing me. He sees that this is uncomfortable ground. But I don't know how to challenge him.

"'Course, back then my own life were different," he sighs, and smacks his lips. "Your Auntie Pam was alive, for one thing."

I nod, and we fall silent for a while. So many dead we have between us. I know what is coming.

He puts his glass on the bar, tilts it slightly. Behind us the slot-machine whistles and ticks, tosses out coins. Uncle Bill leans closer, clears his throat.

"Was it you that found her?" he asks quietly.

"No. She was in Ontario; I live on the other side of the country. In the west."

"Ah," he says, dim memories of geography flickering behind his eyes. "That's right, Vancouver."

I nod again. "She was found by a neighbour. Mum was living in back of a farm house, a small apartment. The woman who owned the place usually gave Mum a ride to work in the morning. When she went to pick her up she noticed the fumes, called her husband over. They had to break the door down in order to get in."

He shakes his head, sucks his teeth quietly.

"The farmer tried mouth-to-mouth, but I guess he gave up on it pretty quickly. I mean, it was obvious that they were too late." I take a quick sip of my beer: bitter.

"Anyway, after that they called the ambulance and the police, and then they called me. I got out there late the next day, soon as I could."

Uncle Bill looks down at his hands, weaves his fingers together. He holds his hands out like that, like he is offering a basket, a gift.

"Did she," he asks, tries again. "Was there a note? Something to explain . . . ?"

"No," I lie. "Nothing." I cannot tell him about the crumpled letter.

He untangles his fingers, reaches into his jacket pocket and pulls out a leather wallet rubbed shiny over time. He opens it, removes some photographs in a yellowed plastic sleeve.

"I knew your mother quite well, you know," he says. "I mean, before she left for Canada." He puts a cracked black and white photograph on the bar. "That's her," he says, "with your Auntie Pam."

Two women sitting on the hood of an old car. One is dressed

in riding gear: knee-high black boots, white jodhpurs, tweed jacket, a helmet. She is looking off to the left, her attention drawn away from the camera. Beside her is a thin woman in a long white skirt and a dark cardigan. My mother, sitting bolt upright and staring directly into the lens as though issuing a challenge. Her left hand is hidden in her right, and both lie limply in her lap.

"It's senseless," Uncle Bill says. I do not look up. "She was a beautiful woman, your mother," he tells me, sniffling slightly, "beautiful and full of life. Then, at least."

Which is why I work in photography, I guess. The *Then at least* behind every picture. The way a photo says both *This is how it was* and *Here it is, still*, at the same time. Time. They knew, the pioneers, that this was about time. Light is time and film is time sensitive.

And why I am here, the *then at least* of my mother's life. Back at my grandmother's house a brass vase on the mantel is full of my mother's burnt and pounded bones. I have come so that we can scatter the ashes in the hills and moors that made up the landscape of my mother's past. Back then, at least.

Uncle Bill drops me off at Grandma's house. When I come in she is still awake, watching TV in the front room. The volume is so high she doesn't hear me come in. On the mantel I can see the urn gleaming like a reproach. I clear my throat.

My grandmother starts, surprised, then glares at me briefly before grabbing the remote control and turning down the TV.

"Did you and Bill have a good chat?" she asks.

"Yes," I answer. "Mostly about Mum, about before she left for Canada." Grandma nods and grunts as she shifts her weight.

"I suppose you must be tired."

"Actually," I say, "I was wondering if you had any old photos, from before Mum left." She looks at me as though puzzled, then gets up slowly.

"Your granddad was never too taken with photographs," she says, and makes her way to the foot of the stairs.

"I'm going to get some sleep," she tells me. "Don't you go staying up too late, we have things to do tomorrow. I expect you'll want to go up the Pike sometime soon, see the reservoirs." She climbs the narrow staircase. At the top: "I'll see if I can't find one or two pictures for you, afterward."

Next morning there is too much to do. Looking around the town, visiting relatives I never knew existed, fighting jet-lag. The photo albums lie somewhere in the house, silent.

A few days later Uncle Bill shows up around ten o'clock, and Grandma and I get into the car. He turns onto the main road that runs through Horwich, west toward Rivington and Chorley. Rough-and-tumble country. If Bill keeps driving straight, an hour could see me in Liverpool staring at where my home lies just beyond the ocean's horizon.

But he turns right, onto a narrow lane lined with rough stone walls that threaten to rip the car wide open. I am the only one who flinches, the only one surprised when we round a bend and startle a pair of sheep standing in the lane. Bill stops quickly, and the ewe bleats up a near-sheer path and into a farmyard. The ram waits for her passage, defiant, then turns a rump clotted with shit toward us and trots away. We are off again.

"Over thur," Bill says, his accent thickening in tune with the landscape, "is Rivington Pike." Points toward a cascade of hills. "With the watchtower." A white stone battlement, solitary and

drowning in tough shocks of grass. Grandma is silent.

Farmhouses, more sheep. On a narrow bridge Bill stops the car, untangles himself from his seat belt. We all get out and walk over to the chest high wall that keeps us from the reservoir. I am carrying the urn. Looking over the edge, I can see another reservoir below, and another, a string of black water.

"Did your Mum ever talk about these reservoirs?" Bill whispers after a while. Wind ruffles the surface.

"Sometimes," I say. "She told me there were houses . . ."

"Aye, at the bottom. When they decided to fill these valleys, to provide water for Rivington and Horwich, they told the people living in them to clear off. The floors and walls of the valleys were lined with rock, and the houses disappeared under water. Last summer, the water got so low you could see the tops of the houses—from a boat, at least."

Buried homes. This is where she should be scattered.

"It's all right," Grandma says, and I only now realize that she is crying, in spite of herself. "She'll be filtered out long before the water reaches town."

I don't understand.

"Each one leads down into the next," Bill explains, "through the rock. The rock filters out any . . . *impurities*." A quick glance at my grandmother.

I open the lid, tilt my mother into the wind.

There is nothing to say. We stand for a minute or two, then get into the car and head for home in silence. On the way back, I decide not to bother visiting Salford.

My grandmother is young and blonde on a stony beach. She is smiling in spite of the small girl beside her, who is trailing a string of seaweed. The child is pointing out to sea.

Schoolchildren in their uniforms, arranged in three careful rows: tallest in the back. In the middle of the bottom row two children—a boy and a girl—hold a small plaque between them: 1943. None of the faces look familiar.

A long-faced young man, already balding, dressed in a baggy suit. My grandfather? He grins at the camera. On his right is my grandmother, smiling decorously. On her lap is a small girl in a floral dress and ankle socks. Her face is turned upward and to her left, toward the man.

I have heard this story. The man in the middle is my grandfather, a long-faced man with a toothy grin, tanned and dusty in his white shirt. Beside him are two short, Indian men, one on each side. This is from the year my grandfather spent in India, working as a welder. He is bringing fresh water and plumbing to a

leper colony. The man on his left has a black triangular hole where his nose should be.

A black dog (a setter?) lying beside two ginger cats reclining like sphinxes and squinting in the sun.

Another picture of three: my grandfather is sitting in an armchair, holding my Aunt Pam in his arms. She lies there, sleeping, wrapped tight in a pastel pink blanket. The photo has been hand-tinted. Granddad's eyes and mouth are wide, his teeth gleaming in his still-tanned face. Beside him, my mother as a girl, her hand on the back of the chair. She is staring directly into the camera (as though offering a challenge?). The smile on her face is thin as a thread. The caption: "My little girl and The Miserable One."

I know what I am looking for, but it isn't here. Maybe it doesn't exist. And maybe it's too late now, anyway. In a few days I have to return to Canada, put my own life back in order.

I had hoped to read in these photos an explanation for what has brought me here. A cast shadow, the arrangement of light that faded long ago. This album is full of formal poses, the com-

memoration of the moment. Snapshots and hints of sibling rival-ry.

There is nothing here to explain why, one Monday morning in late summer day on a small farmhouse in Albion Hills, a stranger should have kicked open a door and released pent-up gas and my mother's last breath into the still early air; why he should have rushed into the kitchen and dragged her cold body out to the yard, where he pressed his mouth to hers and blew useless breath into her lungs. There is nothing here to explain a long-distance call at 3 A.M. from a confused and embarrassed woman in Ontario.

Oh, but I remember flannel sheets orange and warm as tangerines. My mother snaps them out and fills the room with the smell of fresh laundry and a breeze rich with pollen. Because it is so hot she is naked, her skin gleaming with sweat. She snaps the sheets again, slips pillows into bright orange pillowcases. She laughs, tosses the pillows onto the bed like sunburned cheeks.

She sings:

She's a lassie from Lan-ca-sheer

laughs again.

I am hiding inside the wardrobe my father had ordered from England. My mother finds me, smiles. There are lace curtains in the bedroom window but the evening air is heavy and so moist I want to drown in it: there is no breeze. The orange sheets. She calls me My Love, tells me it's time to go to bed. Through the window I can see my father walking up the front steps, carrying a newspaper. Slowly, like he is wading to the door.

There is no story in these fragments, no moral. Only ghosts who passed through rooms and landscapes full of light just long

enough to leave the traces of their movements on sensitive paper. Outlines.

I close the album and turn off the lights.

ALBERT & JULIA

In 1957 Albert Ryan left the slums of Salford and caught the train to Liverpool. He spent the night in a rooming house, and the next morning boarded the *Harmonia* en route to Montreal. The *Harmonia* struggled through the mountains of March waves and arrived in Canada two days later than scheduled.

As soon as the ship docked in Montreal the sky opened and buried the city under an ocean of hard, heavy rain. Albert's worn overcoat was quickly soaked, as were his suit and, finally, the ten dollars he had in his pocket. He knew no one in the city, and other than the address of one of his father's old friends—in Winnipeg—he knew no one in the rest of the country. But still he stood on the dock, waiting for something to tell him where to go or what to do.

He spent the night at the Salvation Army shelter. He couldn't sleep. Beneath him the cot sagged and rolled with the weight of remembered waves; nausea tugged him away from the shores of slumber. He remembered how, when he was young, before he began work as a lathe operator, he had wanted to go to sea with the navy. Flat feet had cut the dream short, but he had at least comforted himself with the knowledge that the metal shavings he left on the shop floor were the by-products of work that gave the ocean-going vessels some of the small parts necessary for their movements. The crossing on the *Harmonia* was the first time he

had been on the sea, and despite the odd bout of seasickness he felt that he had handled the voyage fairly well.

In the morning he bought a postcard and a paper and then went into the first diner he found. Over breakfast he wrote:

> *Dear Julia—*
> *Arived safely in Montreal but wet yesterday. It is a big city I think you wold like it here. Very hot today what a surprise! Right now I am eating brekfast bacon eggs & toast. I will start looking for work today. I miss you very much & cant wait until we are together again my love.*
>
> > *Love*
> > *Albert X X*

In every ad, in each shop and factory window: *No English Need Apply*. He thought of cashing in on his Irish grandparents, masking his accent, but decided against it. He spent his first full day in Canada wandering the city in clothes that were still slightly damp from his arrival.

In the lineup at the Sally Ann he met Peter, a brick-layer from Brixton, who had been in Montreal for two weeks already. Albert's loneliness (to which he would never have admitted) encouraged him to put aside his inherited hatred of Londoners so that he could engage in his first conversation since leaving the ship.

"Fuck all here, mate," Peter told him. "Best bet's to go west. Toronto. Someone'll take you on there."

> *Dear Julia—*
> *I have met a man from London named Peter. Yesterday we arived in Toronto after hitch-hiking for two days it was really rough but worth it because it looks like I might be able to find*

work here. Any day now you will be able to come over & then we
can begin our lives together but until then I will do my best to
make sure that everything is perfect for you here.

All my love
Your Albert X X

The next day (Tuesday) he did find work. He answered an ad for a lathe-operator in a machine shop, but when he arrived at the shop the position had already been filled. The foreman suggested that he try the abattoir across the street. At the slaughter-house the foreman—a ruddy man from Bury—asked him if he thought he could operate the boiler used to cook the ham that was then canned. Albert renounced his career as a lathe-operator and began work that afternoon. By Friday he had found a room on Spadina, and had moved out of the Salvation Army. He offered to let Peter stay with him until he found work, and Peter accepted.

Six months. For six months he stood beside the boiler as it chuffed and hissed; the summer passed in a daze of steam. Overtime became second-nature, as did the lowing and squeals he could almost hear from the killing-floor, behind the drone of the machine. After two months he switched to the night shift for higher pay. During the day the concrete outside his room absorbed the sunlight, poured it through his window and onto the bed where he lay drenched and just this side of sleep; at night, the boiler, the other machines, the heat of the blood and flesh. His life was circumscribed by sweat and exhaustion, his dreams by raw meat and a woman's soft voice heard from far away, as though through a cardboard tube.

Drinking was out of the question back then: every penny, ex-

cept for food and rent, went into his bank account. Even bus fare was considered an unnecessary luxury and so he walked the three miles to and from work each day. By mid-July he had saved enough money that he could write:

Dear Julia—

How are you my love? I hope you are well & are thinking of me as I am of you. It is very hot here in Toronto today how is it in Salford?

Here is a picture I took of the toilet which you will notice is indoors! not like the ones back home. I hope you like the way it looks because it is in your new home that's right I have found a flat for us here. It is only a one bedroom but it is still a start isnt it. I want you to come over as soon as you can please so we can be together again & in our own home at last. At least you wont have to live with your mother and father any more.

I know you have to leave your work & say good bye to everyone but how soon could you be here? I will send a ticket so you don't have to worry about that just go to Liverpool & get on the ship. Only come as soon as you can because I miss you teribly.

Well my dear I will close now so please write back to me soon.

All my love always
Your Albert X X

He said goodbye to Peter, who had found work on a construction site a month earlier, and moved into an apartment on Jane Street. He spent his days and weekends slowly gathering the bits and pieces, pots and pans, dishes and furniture necessary to create a new home. Most of the furniture came from second-hand shops, and one of the chairs was threadbare and subject to dangerous wobbles, but on the whole Albert was pleased and comfortable.

In early August he received his first letter from Julia in almost

five months. She told him how happy she had been to hear from him, but pointed out that it would be better for her to catch a plane to Canada, rather than to make the long journey by ship. A plane could bring her to him in hours, whereas a ship would take days; besides, by plane she could go directly to Toronto, but a boat would only take her as far as Montreal. And, she said, if something should happen to her on the way over (God forbid) she much preferred a quick death in an airplane crash to the long, drawn-out drowning she would face in the event of a shipwreck.

The thought of her body tossed by waves caused Albert to shudder briefly, and convinced him of the logic behind his young wife's argument. He wrote back saying that he would be more than happy to pay for an airline ticket, and booked her a flight for mid-September.

Until then. XX

U ntil then, there was nothing Albert could do but work and wait. August and the last weeks of summer passed quickly, but when September arrived the days were as long and sleepless as they had been in June and July; nights at work dragged on until they seemed to congeal, waist-deep pools through which he had to wade to arrive at the end of his shift.

Because all he did was work, Albert hadn't needed any clothes other than his work clothes. Now, as the day of Julia's arrival

quickly approached, he decided he would have to get a suit: he couldn't greet her at the airport dressed in the greasy trousers and heavily scuffed boots he wore every day.

The day of her arrival was hot and humid. At the airport, Albert stood patiently at the gate through which Julia would appear, although he felt choked by his tie and was perspiring heavily—whether from anticipation or from the weight of his dark woollen suit, he couldn't tell. At seven o'clock Julia's flight arrived; at seven-thirty the doors swung open and she walked out, wrapped in a long, fake-fur coat, her hair concealed by a pale blue silk scarf, protected against the blizzard by which she expected the city to be paralyzed.

What he had hoped for was a sense of reunion, a coming together, connection. He had spent six months more or less alone, strapped to a machine he still didn't really understand. An embrace, then. A moment deafeningly silent as blood pounded in his temples, longing sinking in a still pool. An affirmation.

Julia clicked across the marble floor, placed her hands lightly on his shoulders, brushed his mouth with her lips.

"Oh, Albert," she said, "it was a *horrible* flight. I feel completely shattered."

Back in the apartment, Julia collapsed on the wobbly chair and sobbed into her hands. The furniture, the tiny rooms, peeling paint. Toronto.

"My God, Albert, what have you done to me?"

Albert stared down at his calloused hands, listening to his world crash and whimper around him.

Three months married, six months apart, and now their marriage would begin again: a tentative reclamation of what they had established so briefly before Albert had left.

Three months after they were reunited Julia and Albert bought a car; Julia took driving lessons. By the end of January all their second-hand furniture had been replaced. In March they took out a mortgage on a bungalow outside the city. They turned one of the two bedrooms into a nursery.

But the conception was an accident, a question mark introduced in the wrong part of a sentence. Albert couldn't understand what had changed. He knew that Canada had been a disappointment: Didn't she always talk about Bloody Canadians?

In February Julia had mentioned that she wanted to go back to England to visit her mother and sister. When Albert had complained that it was too expensive she had grabbed a pair of scissors and had locked herself in the bathroom. Panic and anger had helped him to break open the door only to find her sitting on the edge of the bathtub, unharmed. They had made up, as best they could, but Albert was still left taut as a wire for days afterwards.

And then Peter came back into Albert's life. Simply, with a tap on his shoulder in the line at a take-out. Julia had sent Albert around the corner to buy some hot sandwiches, which they often ate in bed while watching TV. Their luxury. Shared this time with Peter, who had come home with Albert to meet Julia.

"At long last," she'd said, "my husband's first friend and saviour." Peter had laughed and then offered her a Red Cap fresh

from the six-pack he was carrying.

"Not like our beer back home," he'd announced, "but still . . . "
Julia had begged off with just the faintest of sniffs.

Albert was becoming increasingly puzzled by Julia's aloofness. He knew Horwich, where her roots were, and knew her family. Not from Salford, clearly, but working class nonetheless. He'd noticed, too, how her accent had shifted after her arrival in Canada—how it had migrated south from Lancashire to somewhere near Oxford and had then moved on to the hazy uniformity of the stage. Airs put on for the colonials?

"Nothing of the sort," she'd replied. "You forget my education, at boarding school. And just because Horwich is a stone's throw from Salford doesn't mean one has to live like a slum-dweller."

And, another time: "My father was a *skilled* tradesman. My mother was the daughter of an officer, raised when Empire still meant something. Don't make the mistake of lumping me with the rag-and-bones-men in your district." So Albert had been chastened, but not silenced.

And Peter had come back into his life.

Albert moved through a bewildering fog, stumbling through the house, bumping into details which loomed from the mist: Julia's anger, Peter's car parked in the street, a cigarette butt floating in the toilet. The world became equivocal—even Julia's hatred of Canada took on a double meaning.

Too long apart, and after too short a time together. He remembered the day Julia had arrived in Toronto, how broken and disappointed she'd seemed. What had she said? *I feel shattered.* Had he been the cause of that, with his awkward speech and

working-class habits? More than once he'd felt ashamed when, while talking with Peter, he'd noticed the smell rising from his clothes, or had compared his own rough and calloused palms with the small clean hands that shook his whenever Peter came to visit. Failure welcomes success.

When the home runs dry, what do you do? Drink. Silence, distance, absence. Hoping, perhaps, that Julia would reach for him in her sleep, would call him from his hiding place.

One day in July Julia struggled for seven hours until, near midnight, their son entered the world. "Dennis," she had said, "Dennis William. After my father." She fell asleep and dreamed of dragging an elephant up a mountain.

At Thanksgiving Peter provided a turkey for dinner. At Christmas he and his fiancée Susan—a brooding, thin-faced woman from Essex—had brought gifts and champagne. This time Julia had not refused, and as a result had endured the humiliation of drunken tears and public vomiting.

Awkward gratitude: without Peter's help the holiday's would have been bare. In spite of what the TV, the car, the new furniture suggested to the world, behind the door of the bungalow Albert and Julia had almost as little money as they had had at the

time of their wedding. Dennis was—and Albert hated himself for thinking it—an added burden they could not, but would, carry.

Peter could afford such generosity. He had found his place in Canada, so much so that he was now a foreman, keeping watch over his former colleagues. The day after Dennis' birth Peter had been there, waving too-large stuffed toys at the wrong baby in the hospital viewing room.

Albert is driving. Julia: "How much do you love me?"

In the back seat Dennis stretches his arms wide. "*This* much!" he shouts. Three years old.

"How much?"

Stretch. "*This* much!"

Albert stares straight ahead. Julia looks out the window as her world rushes past. "Only that much?"

A nd then there was the day in July, when Dennis was five, when Albert came home from work to find Dennis terrified and in tears, Julia laughing. Peter had taken their picture on the front lawn. Everything had seemed oddly perfect then, the house, the landscape, the family. Even the concrete steps which dug into his back as he reclined against them. He wanted to preserve that moment, to always be able to pull it from memory and hold it up

against any present. And then Dennis had told him, and then Albert had asked her, and then the moment was changed forever. He could have torn the photo to shreds.

MALTON—A collision on Airport Road early this morning has left one man dead and two others injured. The accident occurred when the driver of a late model station wagon lost control of his car, which swerved into oncoming traffic and struck a Vauxhall Viva head-on. Rescue workers were unable to revive the driver of the Viva, who was pronounced dead on arrival at Etobicoke General Hospital.

Dead is Albert Ryan, 46, of Rexdale. The driver of the other vehicle is reported to be in stable condition. His passenger was treated for minor injuries and then released.

CORRESPONDENCES

No matter where I am in the city, I can hear the noon horn. Sometimes it sounds like a taunt, sometimes a lament: *O, Canada*. Today it's a lament.

I close the darkroom door on the echoing last note. I make a quick mental check of where everything is—scissors, reel, tank—and turn off the light.

This is the hardest part, the part that has never become second nature. I wait for my eyes to grow accustomed to the dark, and when the ghost-images fade I pop the end cap off the roll of film.

Wednesday, August 4

Dear Dennis,

Have I done something to upset you? Its been so long since I last heard from you, and I get worried sometimes, what with you on the other side of the country. Anyway, if I have upset you somehow, please write and tell me so that I can at least explain.

Even after five years, being in Vancouver is like coming home to find all of your furniture rearranged. Voices, the landscape, somehow the city is at once familiar and alien. To have travelled so far, over mountains and time-zones, to arrive in the same

country. No new currency, no new language.

In spite of my preparations I still have to fumble for the scissors. I cut the film from the spool, trim the end and thread the film onto the reel. As usual, I have to wind it three times, not trusting my judgement in the dark.

I like to take my time in the darkroom. The Hermit. That's what Michelle used to call me. At least once a week I emerge from the dark and chemicals surprised to see the streets grey and cool with first light. Today, by the time I get the negatives into the rinse it's already nearly three o'clock.

When I turn on the safelight I can see the sketch Michelle gave me taped to the darkroom wall: a stork or crane with its long bill half-buried deep in a baby's mouth. The first of her double-edged gifts. She told me that the bird is feeding the child, but sometimes I get the feeling the child is devouring the bird, beak first. A month ago my apartment was full of Michelle's paintings. Portraits smeared with gouache, miniatures behind rough iron bars. One or two works featured my photos, transferred to canvas as part of a huge collage I never really understood. Now, this sketch in the darkroom is all that's left, and I'm wary of its significance.

> *Life here is as dull and depressing as it always is. I dont know what it is, but lately I find myself feeling terribly depressed all the time. I think living in this house is part of the problem. Dont get me wrong, Mark and Karen are simply lovely, but this really isnt the place for me. I need my own place back.*
>
> *Do you remember the front garden, how long your father spent trying to revive those rosebushes? I drove by the house last weekend, when I went to visit your uncle Peter and aunt Susan, and you wouldnt believe the place—the garden is completely overgrown. Even the front steps have been replaced.*

Hunger and the first hints of a headache. I turn on the stereo, and as I make some lunch the apartment fills with music, one of the tapes Michelle made for me when we began seeing each other. *Parakelo*, the singer pleads over Greek rhythms. Please. Foreign lyrics, because Michelle knew I loved the anonymity they offer. The constant trickle of running water as the negatives rinse merges with the music as it traces thin, wavering circles of longing.

When the steam clock on Water Street toots four times I empty the tank, snap the reel apart and hang the negatives to dry.

Geography cannot shake Sunday of its tedium. Even though the streets in Gastown are filled with tourists, the city still feels desolate and stark. Bleached out. Sundays have always had this cast to them, flat and wind-blown.

I can't do anything while the negatives are drying, so I decide to leave the apartment and head over to the North Shore for a walk. The Seabus churns and gurgles past lone cormorants bobbing in its wake.

A few years ago, in Montreal, I saw an exhibit of old photographs. *Leaving Home/Coming Home: The Immigrant Experience*. Ships in the harbour, men in flat-caps and baggy trousers, women in head scarves. In one of the photos I thought I saw my father, years dead, standing with a group of men and smiling so broadly his cheekbones looked like wings beneath his

skin. I couldn't tell for sure: it was one of those group portraits they used to take, pictures of all the passengers gathered at the stern of the ship in mid-ocean. Memento mori. I bought a copy of the catalogue, but when I got home I discovered that this picture was one of the few not included.

What I remember of the photo is the light, the way the water caught the sun and tossed it onto the film. Dad told me that the voyage to Canada was stormy and violent, but there must have been at least one day when the weather was sunny enough to take that portrait. Everything in the picture looked so tentative—the poses, the nervous smiles, home racing further and further away behind the passengers. My father, if it was my father, buoyed up by an incredible smile.

> *I am sorry to hear about you and Michelle. When did you split up? I know I keep going on about this, but arent you at all worried about marriage and raising a family? Maybe its time for you to think about getting a real career, one that will let you settle down and lead a happy life. Youve said yourself that you dont make very much money. Maybe photography is something you should just pursue as a hobby? Then perhaps you wouldnt be so unhappy all the time.*

When I get to the North Shore I buy some day-old bread and slowly walk over to the quay where the tugs gather to berth. Most days there are usually a few ducks or geese in the water, but today there are only seagulls, floating on the small waves or spiralling slowly and warily in the air.

I break a slice of the bread into small pieces and toss some into the water. The gulls are on it instantly, ravenous. Michelle used to hate these weekly visits to feed the birds. "Scavengers," she'd say. "Picking at scraps, living on whatever floats their way." I

think sometimes that was one of the reasons she decided to go back east. She always complained that the only birds in the city were crows and seagulls—carrion-eaters and scavengers, mere survivors.

And you are always so unhappy, Dennis. Of course, you come by it naturally. Your father was always in a foul mood, and you know that I have a tendency towards depression myself. Perhaps these things are hereditary.

Even so, are you sure you need to see a psychiatrist? Ive heard some terrible things about them lately, especially that they can make you remember things in your past that didnt happen. And its not good to dwell on the past. Whats done is done and we just have to accept it, thats what I always say. Surely you cant disagree with that?

I stay in North Vancouver as long as I can, until the sun sets and the city is dotted with pin-pricks of light. It's quieter here, and I'm comforted by the memory of canyons with deep, cold pools of water somewhere up in the mountains behind me. I've only been there once, a few years ago, with a friend who recited Li Po and Trakl from memory as we hiked and scrambled up stony trails. At mid-day we stopped beside the river to eat homemade corn bread, and watched the water rush past like thick, knotted cords. Later we learned that further down river a drowned child had been held underwater by the current for days.

By the time I get back to the apartment darkness has settled in. I go into the darkroom and carefully take down the negatives: some shots of Michelle taken over a month ago, fire-escapes, a long night-exposure of Water Street. At the end of the roll there are two shots I took along the Sea Wall. I cut the film into strips, place the strips on some paper and make a contact sheet. I can

still feel the last traces of the headache from earlier, but I've learned that working in the darkroom seems to keep the pain at bay.

Michelle is looking away from the camera, staring out the window at a grey sky. At the time I thought she was just thinking about her next piece, but looking at the contact sheet I realize how little I understood her feelings. These are photos of departure, of resignation and betrayal.

I work my way through the negatives, printing one shot of Michelle and two of the fire-escapes. The night shot turns out to be slightly out of focus, which has always been my biggest problem. Photography is largely hit-and-miss, one really good shot per roll if you're very lucky.

> *And I think Im also afraid that he will tell you that I was a bad mother, that I didnt give you what you wanted. Promise me you wont talk about me behind my back.*
>
> *Oh, Dennis, I feel so old these days, I find myself looking back on my life and finding something missing, I suppose. You are so far away and unreachable. Thats always been your trouble, you know. You cant be reached by anyone. I hope you dont mind me saying that, but its true.*

In my final year at school we were given an assignment: make a portrait of your family or someone you love, but don't show the people in the shot. An abstract portrait, I guess. I stalled on it as long as I could. At the last minute I threw together some charcoals, a bird's wing, a pine cone and a coyote skull I found in New Mexico a few years back, and arranged them on a map of the world: Michelle. Someone I loved.

Now, however, I realize that I can finally make that family portrait. The last shot on the roll of film shows a rocky beach. In the foreground is a large boulder covered in drying seaweed. In the middle ground a heron balances cautiously on one leg near the shoreline; further out, a tree-stump—driftwood—floats with its roots just above the surface of the water.

> *Im sorry Dennis. This isnt the letter I wanted to write. I wish I could explain. Sometimes I think we all were once capable of doing something important, of making something of ourselves. Now it seems like whatever it was its something we lost sight of a long time ago.*

I make a test strip of the shot, and discover that it's going to be difficult to print properly: if I develop the photo so that the

foreground is clear, the background and middle ground will be too dark; if I concentrate on the stump or the heron everything else is over-exposed. Normally, this wouldn't be such a problem, but this triangle of objects and zones is going to take a lot of dodging and burning. I need to balance the picture, to give each figure equal prominence, equal time. I take the test-strip into the living room to figure it out, and make some coffee. It's almost two o'clock.

> *Please forgive the tone of this letter, I honestly dont know whats wrong with me these days. Maybe I should see a psychiatrist ha ha.*

f8 at eight seconds for the foreground; six seconds for the heron, which still shows up as just a silhouette; $5^{1/2}$ seconds for the stump. Burn in the sky for an extra second. The first time I can't really see any improvement. The second time it looks better but it's still not right: the stump is perfect but the heron got too much light. The third time the exposures are right but the three objects are obviously haloed—too clumsy.

I watch the fourth print swaying back and forth in the tray of developer. The image looms in quickly, slowly picks up details. It looks like this is going to be the one. Then the phone rings. I look at the clock and realize it's after 3 A.M.

*Anyway, my love, take no notice of this. Please just write, even
a quick letter, to let me know whats going on in your life..
Maybe this Xmas I will be able to come out for a visit? Let me
know. Please dont keep this silence with me.*

Take care. Uncle Peter sends his love.

love always, Mum

By the time I get off the phone, the print has burned itself into
total darkness, beyond hope.

THE RESERVOIR

Light. Light from far off and something moving. Waves? Yes, waves, light bouncing on the surface bouncing with the waves. These fronds, slow on my cheeks. Waves.

How fish dart—here; no, there. Fish thin as grass, are they blades of grass? They stop, turn slowly, grow thinner and they are lines in the sky. A sky dappled and light. Light.

Light pushes through her eyelids and floods her dream with pink. When she opens her eyes she sees leaves rustling in the breeze, flashes of light and shadow. Sunday. She lets herself fall back into half-sleep.

A mistake, for when she wakes up the light has pounded its way into her head and lies heavily behind her eyes. Migraine. Beside her, on the bedside table, are a plastic medicine bottle, two-thirds full, a glass of water.

The water is morning-stale, but she is used to this, her morning ritual. Her tongue and palate are dry and sticky; she rinses with a mouthful of water. Then she takes two tablets and lies back against the pillows.

Twenty minutes, a nurse once told her. *Wait twenty minutes, and if you still have the migraine, take two more tablets.* She does, so she does. Her stomach clenches and hardens; codeine sings through

her blood; the muscles in her neck relax and the vertebrae shift. The pain is still there, but it is cold and thin, a metallic taste at the back of the mouth. She gets out of bed.

In the kitchen she fills the kettle with water, puts it on the stove. The hiss of gas reminds her that the pilot light is out, so she gets a match from the cutlery drawer, strikes it and lights the gas. Then she rinses the teapot with hot water and washes her mug from the night before. Through the window she can see Mark and Karen—back from church—as they herd the children out of the car and back into the house. Karen slips her arm around Mark's waist. The ease of such a gesture!

Her thoughts are interrupted by a scratching at the front door. Old Tom, one of the farm cats she has tried to adopt, has come to scavenge what food and affection he can. She opens the door and instinctively steps aside, avoiding the spine and thin tail he tries to rub against her shins. *No more fleas, thank you very much.* Tom pads quickly to the bowl of dry food, tail high as a flagpole. He sniffs the bowl, rubs the side of his face against its edge. She's glad it's him, not that frightening cat without a tail. Rat—an appropriate name, she thinks, and shudders at the memory of the time she touched the finger of bone at the end of his tail stump. To lose a part of oneself, the part that expresses emotion.

It's that loss that repulses her, that makes her more than a little afraid of Rat. *How to tell if he is angry or friendly or indifferent,* she wonders. She gets another glass of water.

In the bathroom she turns on the taps in the bathtub, checks the temperature before she turns to the medicine cabinet and opens it without looking in the mirror. That can wait until after her bath. She opens bottles, shakes a pill (sometimes two) into

her palm and grimaces as each slides down her throat. Then she sits on the toilet while waiting for the tub to fill.

Her husband had bathed so infrequently she had sometimes marked the dates of his baths on the calendar. Until she had realized that he was not bothered. Cleanliness was not part of his nature, nor his class. Where I come from, he would joke, people thought you a toff if you got out of the tub to piss.

She hadn't laughed, of course. She had heard similar stories about the slum-dwellers from her father. And had married into them.

Sometime after she had finally barred her husband from her bed, he began to take baths more often. Shallow baths, that only took minutes to run but in which he would luxuriate for half an hour or more. Once, she had listened at the bathroom door as he sat soaking: gentle splashes, sighs, her name murmured over and over. Then silence, and she had backed quietly away from the door.

She leans back into the water and closes her eyes.

Damn. She should have been more careful, the bath was too hot and now her headache has once again pushed itself into the foreground. She should have expected this. Blood pounding in the back of her neck, her brow, her temples. She goes back into the bedroom, still in her towel, and takes some more painkillers. She takes a quick glance at the alarm clock: just past eleven. Six in two hours.

Too many pills, she thinks, then says out loud. Once or twice a year she used to pour the expired tablets and capsules into the toilet bowl; her son would watch them slowly dissolve away from their rainbow colours before flushing made them spin out of sight. Heart pills headache pills backache pills. Capsules for allergies, tablets for sleep or regularity. She sometimes wonders if there is any part of her body that has not needed some kind of medication. Or, at least, received it. She lies down again and closes her eyes. Presses a pillow tight against the top half of her face.

Once again she feels the return of the cold numb thread of pain. For the rest of the day this will be her obsession, she knows, to

keep the headache at bay. Even if she finds something with which to occupy herself, she will still withhold a part of herself, the part that is keeping a cautious eye on the pain.

And the discomfort of that obsession will itself become an obsession. She knows that she will have to endure the nausea, the desolation that comes from having taken so many painkillers. But that can't be helped. And since Peter isn't coming over after all, she can afford the luxury of drowsiness.

Around noon she decides to make herself something to eat, even though her body tells her not to. In the kitchen she beats two eggs, adds chopped mushrooms and some spring onion. She turns on the gas and lights the burner.

While she is eating the omelette there is a knock on the door and Karen enters carrying a baking tin covered with silver foil. Karen is suspicious of her migraines, has in fact said that they're caused by stress (which is the same as calling her a hypochondriac, isn't it?) or diet. So she decides not to mention the headache which even now threatens to rise again. Brownies, Karen tells her, lifting her gift slightly. And, of course, the rent. She gets her purse, rummages around until she finds her chequebook. Karen accepts the cheque, albeit while turning her head away. She likes to be above such things.

After Karen leaves, she decides to write the letter she's been putting off for three days now. She gets a pen, some paper, and sits at the kitchen table.

Sunday August 22

Dear Dennis,

I am afraid this will have to be a rather short letter, as I am suffering from yet another migraine, its the third one this month and I honestly dont know why Ive been getting so many.

I cant say I was very happy to receive your last letter. In fact, to be honest, it upset me a great deal. I dont know why you feel you have to hurt me like this, perhaps as you say it is because of this "therapy" youre doing, but it just isnt fair. You know all about what happened between your father and I and I dont know why you feel it necessary to bring dreams and fantasies into it.

Because thats what it is, fantasies. You remember no such thing because no such thing ever happened. If, as you claim, you have these "memories" it is because your father has poisoned your mind against me and that is all there is to it.

Its true that I never loved your father—although I thought I did I actually just felt sorry for him—but I was never unfaithful to him in the ten years of our marriage.

This won't do. She crumples the letter into a tight ball, places it on the table beside her, and looks out the kitchen window to where Karen's laundry snaps on the line.

She remembers orange sheets. Cotton, because it was so hot that summer. Orange sheets as cool to lie between as tangerine on the tongue. She'd made them herself, and the colour was tangerine.

That afternoon he surprised her, and they didn't have much time. They raced upstairs to the bedroom and undressed quickly, their bodies sweating and glistening in the light from the afternoon sun crashing through the window.

Wait, she whispered, *I'll put the new linen on the bed*. She snapped the sheets out, slipped the pillows into their cases and tossed them onto the bed. Singing under her breath:

She's a lassie from Lanc-a-sheer

and laughing. In the doorway Peter laughed too, then slipped his arms around her waist. *Fuck me*, she said, surprising them both. They kissed and fell on the bed. The orange sheets.

There was a lace curtain hanging limp at the window: no breeze. They could have drowned in the heat, could have swum through each other's bodies they were so slick from their efforts. Her hair soaked and tangled beneath her head, strands caught in their mouths as they kissed. She whispered, *My Love!*

The bed squeaked and creaked and then she noticed it wasn't the bed but the door to the wardrobe. *Dennis*.

You spying little bastard! she hissed, yanking him out from where he had been hiding. And slapped him, hard, again and again.

And then a whistle from outside. Albert had come home, was walking up the steps to the front door. Slowly, as though wading through the heat. Peter was up and already getting dressed.

Dennis was crying. She stopped slapping him, yanked his face up to hers, shook him. *Don't you dare breathe a word of this to anyone*, she spat, and wiped her mouth with the back of her hand.

She runs the back of her hand across her mouth and looks out the kitchen window to where Karen's laundry flaps on the line. Her headache has returned, snapping in sympathy with the sheets and shirts. Failed love and new love—how do you explain these things to a child?

But Dennis did tell, not then but later that day. They'd handled Albert's arrival well. Peter had rushed into the bathroom, and she had made Dennis help her to remake the bed. By the time Albert had arrived at the bedroom only the heavy scent of sweat and Dennis's tear-soaked face remained to betray her, and both had been easily explained away.

They'd all gone outside to escape the heat. Dennis had taken his plastic shovel and had gone to sulk by the hedge; Albert had sat on the front steps while Peter took her picture. Somewhere there is a picture of that day.

It wasn't until much later, after Peter had gone home, that she'd overheard Dennis whispering in his room; then she had heard Albert's voice, full of stumbles and long silences. When he had confronted her with the accusation she'd responded with indignation, had refused to discuss it. He had believed her, had apologized, but she now found herself wondering just how much of it he had in fact believed. But it certainly hadn't changed their marriage at all. And she had never forgiven Dennis.

Ohhh and this headache is getting to be too too much. She goes

into the bedroom, looks at the alarm clock: 2 P.M. Two more tablets. She could be an animal gnawing through her own leg but she *must* escape this trap. All this dwelling on the past—what does it give but pain, anyway, and hasn't she had enough of that? *Damn Dennis.* She really thought he'd forgotten that day, and now he has to go dragging it all up again. Still, he doesn't really remember all of it, thank God, claims he only remembers something about Peter and her and a wardrobe. And those damned sheets. Maybe in time he'll put this aside, concentrate on other things.

Outside, the air is warm but comfortable, not the treacle she imagined it would be today. A walk is what she needs, go down to the pond and watch the ducks. At the edge of their property Mark has filled a large, deep hole with water—the pond. In summer she can usually find ducks there, either on the water or hiding in the reeds that have grown at its edge. Although they prefer her to keep to her part of the property, Mark and Karen tolerate, but don't encourage, her visits to the pond. At least once a week she can be found there, sitting on "her" rock, watching nothing happen.

But she is out of luck today: no ducks. Just as well, since she doubts her head could handle the shimmering green hoods, the flashes of blue on their wings. And, she has to admit, she is feel-

ing more than a little dazed. Lowering herself to her rock is in itself a trial. But she endures.

Back then she had imagined that Peter was the one true love of her life, the one to whom she was spiritually bonded. A heroic love in the face of sorrow and the impossible. Now ... Peter came to visit when he could, and there were still vague hints about his unhappiness with Susan, but she had given up on that kind of hope.

When she was a girl her father used to ask her, *How much do you love me?* and she would open her arms almost farther than they could reach: *This much, Daddy!* That was the sort of love she had imagined, love beyond reason. She had always felt that she was destined for something great, a faint, shimmering blessing on the horizon. Just beyond reach. Or a tragic gesture, renunciation perhaps. Yes, to renounce the world for some higher cause; to suffer because she was, oh, so far beyond not suffering. Love and suffering.

She thought of a statue of a woman (a saint, maybe?) she had seen in a book at boarding school: an angel smiles sweetly as he drives a spear through the folds of marble dress and into the heart beneath. And the ecstasy on the woman's face! Suffering lifting her high into the air, piercing her even as she is welcomed into the embrace of a billowing, divine cloud.

She wakes with a start. Looks over her shoulder to make sure no one has been watching her. There is a slight rustle of curtains back at the house. Karen?

She tries to concentrate on the water. What was that dream? Ah, now she remembers: she was lying on the bottom of the reservoir in Horwich, her back resting on rough stones, watching

the sunlight swim down from where it danced on the water's surface.

She'd seen it, once, when she and her father had gone into Horwich for the afternoon. They'd walked through Rivington and had climbed Rivington Pike to the old watchtower at the top. She had wanted to keep going, to head toward Winter Hill and further into the moors, but a storm had forced them to crouch at the base of the tower until the clouds and rain had blown past them. By that time, they had had to begin their descent back to the village.

Her father had suggested they descend by way of the reservoirs. Rams scattered on the trail before them, the wool around their rumps and balls clotted with dung.

He told her that at the bottoms of the reservoirs there were houses which had been abandoned when the little valleys had been lined with stones in anticipation of the rains which would fill them. Some years, he told her, when there's been no rain, the water sinks and sinks until you can see the roofs of the cottages. She wondered to herself if anyone still lived there, dreaming watery dreams on a flooded pillow. And this morning she had done just that.

A fter dinner, she still feels dazed and tired. Tea, she thinks. Stumbles to the kitchen, where she fills the kettle, turns on

the burner and gets the matches from the cutlery drawer. A chill rushes over her, and she walks to the bedroom to get a pullover. She comes back to the kitchen and sits at the table, waiting for the kettle to boil.

She looks out the window, past her reflection and into the darkness where she can see that Karen has taken in the laundry. Already, she imagines, the children are lying between crisp orange sheets, the room filled with the scent of fresh laundry and August wind. Unlike this room, its sharp scent of gas.

She begins to doze and slips into a warm dark place where sound is low and muffled, rubbing itself against her ears. The air undulates with the movement of small waves high up on the surface.